Praise for Emily Forever

"Emily is nineteen years old, works at the supermarket, and is pregnant. Her boyfriend Pablo has gone out 'to sort something out' and hasn't returned. Her mother, who raised Emily alone, moves into the little apartment to help. *Emily Forever* is a properly defiant novel. It refuses to be categorized. Yes, it deals with class and poverty, but it's just as much about the way we look at the so-called poor and powerless. Maria Navarro Skaranger has written an intelligent, ironic, vital, and poetic novel, which with its many changes of narrative perspective challenges the reader's expectations and ideas. With its defiant attitude, Skaranger reminds us that the story of the passive, drowsy, and not very future-oriented Emily is very much one worth telling."
Jury, the Critics' Prize (Norway)

"Skaranger writes with wisdom and heart about the anybodies of society in this brilliant novel. Skaranger is a glowing literary talent, and part of what makes this novel so rich is its inquiring, critical, observing narrative voice."
Dagens Næringsliv

"A profoundly beautiful book about a rudderless existence that seems genetically conditioned. Skaranger's warm prose and deeply felt sympathy for Emily glows throughout the novel."
Dagbladet

"In beautiful, intuitive prose, Maria Navarro Skaranger shows how class contempt is expressed in Norway. A fantastic book."
Vårt Land

"In a novel distinguished by intelligence and nuanced prose, Maria Navarro Skaranger follows her confused main character into a new life phase. Her body of work exudes a peculiar, beautiful energy."
Klassekampen

"There are many reasons why *Emily Forever* is a fantastic book. To me, the narrative voice is the most important; it is the means through which Maria Navarro Skaranger approaches her main character, a poor nineteen-year-old girl who is about to become a single mother, with a peculiar mix of closeness and distance— and also wonder, tenderness, and subtle humor."
ULLA SVALHEIM, *Vårt Land*, Best Books of 2021

"I have read many novels about class, class journeys, and social inequality over the past year. Many of them have been good, but none have woven together the structural and the individual, the political and the existential, as elegantly as Maria Navarro Skaranger does in *Emily Forever*. A gorgeous book!"
INGEBORG MISJE BERGEM, *Vårt Land*, Best Books of 2021

"This might very well be how the world is for 'the girl at the check-out counter at the supermarket,' who parents use to scare their children with when they refuse to do their homework. Skaranger portrays such a woman for better or worse. She hopes with her,

struggles with her, breathes with her. It is deeply moving."
MARIANNE LYSTRUP, *Vårt Land*, Best Books of 2021

"Maria Navarro Skaranger's books are full of beautiful, fallible people, portrayed with honesty and love. Emily—nineteen and about to become a mother—is no exception. The Oslo writer's effortless, vivid prose suits this book about growing up faster than you might want to."
ELIAS BAKKEN JOHANSEN, *Vårt Land*, Best Books of 2021

"A powerful, sharply written novel about finding value in the life you have."
Adresseavisen

"Skaranger's third novel hits the mark. *Emily Forever* is a novel about a young soul in a terrifying situation, written with integrity and a distinctive approach. Skaranger draws up young characters in the beautiful/ugly landscapes of East Oslo with an impressive lightness and authenticity."
NRK

"Again, it's Skaranger's distinctive literary sense that makes this book shine. The author portrays pregnancy, birth, and the postnatal period with her very own vitality, irony, and poetry. Her alertness to the material details of class differences is perhaps at its highest in *Emily Forever* and is accompanied by a finely tuned depiction of caregiving. With literary authority Maria Navarro Skaranger has succeeded in writing a tight, short novel rich in themes and motives. In this way she

assumes her place among the greats with confidence and a great naturalness."
MARGUNN VIKINGSTAD, *Morgenbladet*

"*Emily Forever* makes room for a person who isn't usually included in language and literature. What makes it so magnificent is that Maria Navarro Skaranger refrains from turning Emily into a representative for this or that. When I read the novel for the third time, I realized that I had to let go, but also that the ice-cold times we live in produce a desire for living literature. Emily. Look at her and make up your own mind."
Dagens Nyheter, Sweden

"What makes *Emily Forever* into something absolutely out of the ordinary is the way that the omniscient narrator wanders in and out of the characters, rendering their thoughts and experiences unwaveringly solid and doubtful at the same time. It actually feels like Navarro Skaranger has invented a new and irresistible way of portraying people."
Aftonbladet, Sweden

"Skaranger shows the control she has over her craft. With apparent simplicity she gets under the skin of the novel's characters, at the same time precisely pointing out how poverty isn't just about material things. There are glimpses of brutal humor but the tone is serious and between the lines you sense a tender, trembling indignation, which also spreads to the reader, coalescing into a knot in the stomach."
Svenska Dagbladet

"Skaranger writes about pregnancy, motherhood, and often-unheard people's inner lives in a way that feels unique and pioneering. Everybody wants to tell stories about class these days, but it's rarely done in such an unpretentious way. The perspective shifts from one character to the other, always seamlessly. I don't understand how Navarro Skaranger does it, how the author herself can reach into Em's existence and speak directly to the reader, but she does, and it's completely natural and very elegant. A moving, laconic little novel which seems to say more than the words it contains."
Borås Tidning

Emily Forever

MARIA NAVARRO SKARANGER

Emily Forever

Translated from the Norwegian
by Martin Aitken

WORLD EDITIONS
New York

Published in the USA in 2024 by World Editions NY LLC, New York

World Editions
New York

Printed by Lightning Source, USA

This book is a work of fiction. Any resemblance to actual persons, living or dead, or actual events is purely coincidental. The opinions expressed therein are those of the characters and should not be confused with those of the author.

Library of Congress Cataloging in Publication Data is available

ISBN 978-1-64286-137-2

First published as Emily Forever in Norway in 2021 by Forlaget Oktober, Oslo

This translation has been published with the financial support of NORLA.

Company: worldeditions.org
Facebook: @WorldEditionsInternationalPublishing
Instagram: @WorldEdBooks
TikTok: @worldeditions_tok
Twitter: @WorldEdBooks
YouTube: World Editions

POOR EMILY

Winter, and dark nearly all day, in the mornings until ten. Emily (Em? Or Emma, perhaps?) wakes up with the light, it's late for her.

Look at her, lying with a pillow between her legs and one hand on her tummy, her eyes looking towards the window, looking out of the window; it's grey out today. Emily, such a sad name for anyone to have, so heavy with rain that an elderly aunt would have smoothed her hand over the girl's hair and said, you poor child, are you here in this flat on your own? Time to get up, Emily, her aunt would have said, and so she rises, and the bed sheets smell of something more than just her, she has to roll out of bed because of her tummy, late, it's late, her body is almost like a brick now, she feels rectangular, broad across the back, bulky, fluid in her ankles, her face is too flat and too round.

She looks at herself in the mirror, and there's her father, in her nose, her skin, the thickness of her wrists, her mother's in her hair. Emily doesn't want to think about it, she puts on some trousers and a sweater.

Her flat's very small, room enough for two but no more than that, not really. A small living room, a bedroom with a bed in it, and under the bed some storage for clothes now dumped in a pile against the wall because she can't be bothered folding them and putting them away (her clothes are always creased now, it makes her look unkempt even though she keeps herself clean). A small kitchen, a small table with two chairs, walls that separate the rooms, washing machine in the basement. She spends many minutes and hours lying in bed, staring at the wall and the ceiling in the darkness of night, and because she sleeps so little the TV will be on for hours when she doesn't have to go to work. She turns it on as soon as she gets up and it has to stay on all day with the volume on 33 so she doesn't have to have any thoughts of her own, just looking at the breakfast programme with that foodie guy frying a big white piece of fish is enough to make her thoughts jump off the balcony and smack down on the concrete below before making off.

Now she looks at her phone and it says MAMMA has called three times, and a minute after the third call MAMMA has sent a text message: Hello are you awake, give me a shout when you see this. A person can't go around being scared of their own mother (the way mothers are scared of their daughters), not when a mother is the only thing they've got, because Em hasn't got anyone else but her old mum, not now, but she feels (the hairs of her arm standing on end) that she'd better reply at once so that her mum won't be worried. She presses the number and knows her mum'll wait a while before answering, and if Em hangs up before her mum answers, her mum might very well tell her: Don't hang up so quickly, it can start me off crying.

After thirty seconds (Em counts them as it rings), her mum picks up the phone.

Em asks why she called, and her mum says she was thinking of going out today and was wondering if Emily needed anything doing, she could get some shopping in for her. Em asks her what she was thinking she might need doing. Not to be cheeky, though that's how it's taken, and her mum says, What do I know, and Em thinks of what she might need doing, she can't think of anything other than maybe changing the light bulb in the bathroom. She tells her mum she can come over around fourish if she wants, and her mum says, yes, she will.

Emily, that poor girl. Today, on this very day, she's been pregnant for seven whole months, and it's just the two of them now, Em and her ever-swelling tummy, Em and the baby, after Pablo disappeared out the door to sort something out, as he put it. Yes, that's what he did, disappeared. Or was it? There's something I need to do, he said, and locked himself in the room for two hours with the key, Em was sitting on the sofa watching TV, she fell asleep, woke up, Pablo was still in the room, and then he went out the door, with a black holdall hanging from his shoulder. Em looked at Pablo before he went, Pablo looked at her, Em wondered what Pablo was thinking, where he was going, Pablo winked at Em, went out the door, locked it behind him, and Em carried on watching TV.

She waited up the first few nights, listening out for the lift or footsteps on the stairs, listening for cars stopping outside the block. Later she calls him again, calls and calls, until he answers. His voice is without emotion. What's going on, she wants to know, and Pablo says, Nothing, his voice is so detached, and Em says, Nothing, what's that supposed to mean, and Pablo says, I don't know, and then, after a long pause, I need some time on my own, and there's something I need to sort out with Ousman. Em drums her fingers against the pane, she says, On your own, what's that supposed to mean, and Pablo says, It means I think it's best we're apart for a bit, and Em doesn't grasp this, that he's dumping her, or else she doesn't want to grasp it, no, she doesn't get it at all, she thinks he needs to get this something sorted out with Ousman and that after that, at some later time, he'll phone her, but who knows.

There are moments now and then when Emily perhaps understands that she's been abandoned, but only moments. If you look at her then, her eyes become big and dark and tired (a person gets so incredibly tired when they've been abandoned), she looks quite distraught.

But when she finds twenty thousand kroner in a carrier bag under a pillow in the bedroom and has counted it all, her eyes light up again.

That elderly aunt would have said: But my dear child, these things happen, and she would have held Emily and rocked her gently from side to side, and Emily would have fallen asleep again.

And then she'd wake up, and you'd look at her and feel like asking: So what do you want to be when you grow up?

At some point, Em's mum told Em she'd have to start earning her own money if she wanted hairbands and makeup like the other girls (her mum was always so skint by the end of the month that Em would have to phone and ask if it was all right to take something from the fridge when she was on her own at home). And at some later point, Em walked into a supermarket with a printed CV and a job application, and that's how she got her first job.

New black tarmac has been laid outside the block, a dark path with a handrail all the way from Em's entrance down to the metro station where she takes the train into work, early early she goes out the door (she can hardly go out the door without someone looking at her) and keeps hold of the handrail all the way to the platform so as not to slip on the ice, early early she starts work at the supermarket to get everything ready. Open up, switch the cash registers on, the ATM. Marewan logs on to his computer, he makes a smoothie too, and goes to the loo, while Em puts the kettle on and makes herself a coffee. Em lugs the bundled newspapers inside, puts VG and Dagbladet and Aftenposten out on the racks, along with a couple of other smaller papers. Marewan puts a chair out behind the boxes of apples, Em sits down and catches her breath, it's time for what Em likes best about the job, which is checking the fruit. She checks for little imperfections, nicks in the apples, splits in the bananas, avocados that are too soft, some of the customers will squeeze an avocado flat just so they can get twice the amount refunded. She makes a pyramid of the oranges, picks a few leaves from the cabbages and some from the basil, and then she sits down again.

Em checks and checks, until her eyes are tired by the yellow strip lighting on the ceiling, until Marewan asks her to take the waste items out then go to the checkout.

At some point, before her break, as she neatens the newspapers on the racks into fat rectangles, she sees a small photo of Pablo's friend Ousman in a corner of one of the front pages. She opens the newspaper and reads, in a very brief article, that police have raided the home of a key figure in Oslo's criminal community, that figure being Ousman, and found there a person with serious injuries, near-comatose in a bed, along with a lot of drugs. It asks anyone with any information to come forward and contact the police.

She reads with wide eyes and her mouth agape, she looks so stupid but the feeling she has isn't unpleasant, more one of excitement, as if she'd seen her own name in the paper. Marewan says, What are you up to? Em says, Nothing, and puts the newspaper aside so she can read it again later on. She calls Pablo's number while sitting on the loo, only he's not answering.

It's morning, the shop has just opened when Mare-wan, the boss, checks up on the other stores in the franchise, how much they're selling, some are showing a turnover of almost four million. Mare-wan's met some of the others who run the stores, young, ambitious, often homosexual men who've chosen to put off going to university because they can earn up to several million a year as store manager, or even as assistant store manager, in super-market retailing. His own turnover is substantial, but not that substantial, he'd like it to be more, but there's a lot of shoplifting goes on, and Marewan is tired of shoplifters, tired of the days that keep coming, one after another, and tired because he hasn't yet finished his smoothie, his eyes are stiff at the corners from lack of sleep. He prints out three sheets of A4, photos of shoplifters, fixes them to the door of the cold store and writes on them in felt pen, Thieving Kurdish mafia, exclamation mark. It's Kurds who're doing the stealing, Marewan believes, some steal jams and marmalades, jars slipped into their bags, others beer, cans slipped into theirs, and Romanians steal too, or Bulgarians, they don't only have to come from Romania. Marewan has seen the big 4x4s parked outside in the street, with BG on the plates. The Pakistanis aren't thieves, but they're lots of other things, Marewan thinks, so you've got to watch out for them too.

He puts a notice up about the staff get-together, which is also a farewell do for Emily before she goes on maternity leave, he's booked everyone in to go tenpin bowling in the city centre, they'll meet at the shop first, a minibus will take them into town to bowl, then they'll come back to the shop and park outside before going on to a good local restaurant for a slap-up meal. It's important they put their names down in good time, Marewan's written on the notice.

Now Emily's out in the aisles sticking security tags on all the beer cans, she's sitting on a chair with fridge gloves on and she'll be tagging for hours.

Marewan feels a certain responsibility for Emily, not the way a father or brother would, or even a boyfriend, maybe more like a store manager whose employee she is? This sense of responsibility comes up in him when a male customer Marewan's clocked as a shifty type comes into the shop and asks Emily to show him where the sugar is, and even though Emily can hardly walk and must waddle from side to side, the flats of her hands pressed to the small of her back, she has to lead the customer nearly all the way to the far end of the shop, to the second shelf under a sign that says Baking Items, where she bends down and picks up a packet of sugar she then gives to the customer, who tells Emily she's almost as sweet herself. Marewan comes and takes over then, helps the customer, tells Emily she can go on a break, and afterwards, at the checkout as she buys a coke and some crispbread, Em says, You saved me there, Marewan.

And Marewan feels the urge then to use her nickname, Em Em Em, the way Tina does. He just doesn't know how.

Before Marewan calls it a day, he scans the books. The first days of the week, Monday, Tuesday, and Wednesday, were quiet, apart from when people were getting off work, they took in a lot of money then, but when the weekend came things took an upturn and they landed on 601, more than the 558 he'd estimated in the budget, which is good, because looking ahead the turnover seems set to stabilise at 600. But Marewan sees too that the staff are giving refunds on a certain brand of cream cleaner and on a number of more expensive items as well, in one case last month it was eight boxes of blue grapes at almost fifty kroner the box, as well as a number of air fresheners, it's Emily, but not just Emily, she's being generous because she's pregnant, it's several of the staff who've been doing it, giving refunds to the customers. He steps out of the office into the shop and tells Emily, who's locking up today, that it's a scam and that from now on all items covered by the Fruit & Veg Guarantee need to be okayed by him first, even if the amount's under a hundred kroner. Emily tells him it was one of the angry ones, most likely on their way to the social security office, she didn't know what to do, she was the only one there at the time, Jørgen was on his break from the checkout. Give me a shout, always, Marewan says. It's a technique the drug addicts use, they'll nick an item off the shelf and ask if we'll take it back. That's why you always need to see a receipt and check it carefully, Marewan says. Apart from that, it's all just the usual, Emily has to take the bread out half an hour before closing, and the other baked goods, to put in the waste skip, she has to ask whoever's on the checkout to tidy the shelves, toothbrushes and the like, bundle the unsold newspapers, replenish the cigarettes and other tobacco products.

Marewan posts the weekly super job too. This week it's helping him put up a display for Asian specialty products.

After that, Marewan's in his car, sitting in the tailback on Trondheimsveien, on his way back home to his housing block, or else he's on the E6 on his way home to Lørenskog or somewhere else out there, Ellingsrud perhaps, on his way home to his wife, his dinner, a shower, and then bed, lights out.

Emily sends him a text after her shift, it's gone one in the morning, it says, I can't come to the get-together, Marewan texts her back straight away, But it's for your sake we're doing it, and Emily replies, I've got something on with family, enjoy yourselves.

After that, anyone could get the idea Emily's a strong and unambiguous woman, but no, Emily is weak weak. She's weak in her body, because she's pregnant (and soon she'll be off sick as well), her legs are thin thin, her head hangs forward. And weak in her person too, vague and ill-defined, and all this is why Marewan has put a chair out for her at work.

She has to sit on the chair nearly all day because of her pelvis, she daydreams on her chair, and what might she be thinking about? Well, probably nothing, until a customer's standing in front of her asking if they've got Pavlova cake, and Em asks him if he means frozen Pavlova cake, only the customer doesn't know, his wife just gave him a list. I don't think we have, she says. Among other memorable customers there's another one today who wonders why she always looks so sad, or sullen (the customer doesn't know the difference between sad and sullen), she looks like she's not happy to see the customers, not even the regular ones who shop there every day, she ought to smile a bit more.

A few days ago Em fell asleep on her break, flopped over the table, her head resting on her arm, or her cheek against the table surface, her belly jammed underneath, and after forty minutes Marewan came in. He shook her gently by the arm and said break time was over.

It's a lot quieter than usual, there's only the shower water running, and everything's so much worse then, because when it's quiet she's forced to think, long and convoluted thoughts, thoughts on top of thoughts on top of thoughts, all queueing up and never stopping. She washes her armpits with soap, and under her breasts, her crotch and the back of her neck, she rinses herself and turns the water off. Now she's all wet and the bathroom's cold, water seeps from the shower cabinet onto the floor, she steps out into a puddle on the floor and thinks, a sudden distressing thought, that she's having a baby that'll grow up in a home where the shower cabinet leaks, a home with smudges of fake tan formula on the door frame, oh no.

Does she feel abandoned? At first she cried her eyes out, then after a while she'd cried so much she couldn't remember why, and everything fizzled out. But can she really just pick him away, like a crusty dark scab on an old midge bite?

Is her inner world so much bigger than the one that surrounds her?

Yes, she's thinking about Pablo's face, the mole on his cheek, his yellow hue.

At night she dreams about faces and bodies and about snuggling up close, and now and then, when she lies there long enough with her eyes closed, she manages to conjure up an actual feeling of Pablo being there with her. Em feels that Pablo's actually there.

Pablo used to put his hand on her tummy, her flat tummy, and Pablo would smooth his hand in circles, round and round her belly button. There's a little Pablo in there, Pablo would say, and was quite certain it was a boy.

But now anyone would have said it was time for Em to move on, they'd have said it looks like Pablo's not going to be coming back. But how do you end a relationship with someone you can't get in touch with? It can't be done. Write a note? A text?

There are things Emily knows nothing about, things about Pablo, things that are none of her business, that she doesn't delve into.

Pablo phones and says he doesn't want anyone, whether it's Em, Em's mother,or anyone in Pablo's family, making any kind of statement to the police, he doesn't want anyone even saying a word to the police. The pigs'll make out they're your mates just to get you talking, Pablo says. They'll do for you rather than help you, Pablo says. Ask for a solicitor, Pablo says. But what have you done, asks Em. Nothing, Pablo almost yells back. And so the first time she's interviewed by the female police officer Em'll ask for a solicitor even though they're sitting in two armchairs and there's just a low table between them with a potted plant made of plastic on it. The policewoman will give a wry smile, because Em sounds like she's saying something she's got from watching films. We're just having an informal chat, yet now you say you want a solicitor, the policewoman will say. That surprises me a bit, don't you think you should just tell me what you know?

Emily, as grey and as wet as the concrete housing blocks up at Romsås, how's she going to manage taking care of a child? Can she look after a kid, will it come naturally to her, or will she stiffen completely?

There're always going to be families who can't manage, in some families calamity is handed down through the generations, it's in their DNA, tucked inside them, working away. This is underlined everywhere Em goes, it's marked with a cross on her health card, after three appointments at the health centre without the child's father turning up the midwife saw no option but to write Alone with child in the column for other relevant information, even though her tummy's growing the way it's supposed to and the baby's heart is beating normally. And then there's the doctor, who says pelvic pain is something that can get a lot of people down and make them depressed. It makes it hard to get enough exercise. Exercise is important, he says, and it's especially important to be active during pregnancy. It's important that you come back and see me if you start feeling down in the dumps. It'll all get better gradually, the doctor says, and the next morning already, at 9 a.m., the family centre (or whatever it's called) phones and says they've spoken to Em's doctor and are all prepped and ready to help at short notice should they be required. It's a low threshold service, the woman on the phone says, in case you need someone to talk to. And although the woman on the phone does her best to make her voice sound kind and considerate, as if she's smiling throughout, she knows it's only a matter of time before the pregnant woman she's talking to collapses in on herself like a cheap folding chair. Em tells her everything's fine, that she's fine, which often she feels she is.

She's put on several kilograms in the space of a week and the midwife at the health centre will say straight away that Em's big now and if Em doesn't get a move on they'll have to induce the birth before she's due, her pelvis is too narrow, or no, it's because such big babies are a risk (but that's got nothing to do with the pelvis, I don't know why she says this to Emily).

Em has spread and takes up more space than she wants to, she takes up two seats on the metro with her thighs splayed out. But now the idea of having a baby is something she's grown comfortable with, the baby's there inside, waiting for me, says Em. It's good you're now making room for the baby mentally, says the midwife. She asks Em to lie down on what to Em looks more like a table, only it's an examination couch the midwife has covered with paper towel. The paper crackles as Em lies down on it and the midwife is warm and kind now, she warms the gel in her hands and rubs it all over Em's tummy and then listens in various places, not there, but here, here's the baby's spine, the midwife says, and runs the listening apparatus down her left side, she presses the apparatus gently against Em's tummy a couple of times, causing the baby to move, to roll around. After that, she measures with a measuring tape and says, This big.

Yes, at first the midwife is warm and kind, but then she switches to serious, the midwife is like a light switch turning on and off, she taps the keys of her computer with small, slender, wrinkly fingers whose nails are varnished pink. She's spoken to Em's doctor and she's spoken to the family centre and she's spoken to a social worker about follow-up, they can put some hours aside for her on Wednesdays, or they can phone, so that someone's there for her to fall back on, so that someone's got her back, the midwife says. And you must mind the sugar, no sugar, and keep your legs high.

Besides that she ought to be on full sick leave. The midwife wonders why she isn't (listen my dear, listen petal), hasn't her boss noticed she's pregnant, she can't be this heavily pregnant, in her third trimester, and be working full-time in a supermarket (!). But what does Emily know, all she's done is take on fewer shifts because she's been tired and feeling sick. I see, says the midwife, question is how much parental benefit you'll get.

Like a saving angel the neighbour comes darting towards Emily's mum who's standing outside the entrance door of the housing block, he breaks into a trot and comes towards her, Em's mum, she looks a bit decrepit, clutching an empty-looking carrier bag in her hand, without a hat or scarf. Let me get that for you, the neighbour says, and Em's mum smiles, he opens the door for her and holds it wide. She goes inside and stamps the snow off her shoes on the mat next to the letter boxes. Now there's a gentleman, says Em's mum, and starts to climb the stairs. The neighbour asks if she wouldn't prefer to use the lift, and Em's mum says, The lift, no, I never use the lift. I'd been waiting quite a while outside, a good job you came. My daughter lives on the top floor, she never hears the bell, I don't think she wants to, Em's mum explains, then adds with a laugh, Now she'll wonder how I got in. The neighbour follows her up the stairs, agreeing with everything she says, You're right there, very true, and it takes an age because Em's mum goes so slowly, anyone would think she was an old woman. When they get to the third floor, he says, Cheerio then, and say hello, and the mother of the girl called Emily acknowledges this with a little wave.

Em's mum has come to change the light bulb, at long last Em sent her a text saying it had gone (she lied and said it had gone the night before, whereas the fact of the matter is it's been dark for two weeks) and that she needed someone to watch out for her when she was standing on the chair, in case she fell.

What a tip, says Em's mum, who hasn't been inside the flat for quite a while. And, well, she'd probably been expecting the place to be more ... spotless (?), it being a young woman's flat and all. But before she goes in she stamps the snow off her shoes on the doormat (again), then takes them off and puts them down neatly beside each other in the hall. A tip, yes, that's about right, Emily thinks to herself. But then she thinks it's just something her mum's saying, because her mum wants to tidy up. It's not that bad, is it? Em says, and Em's mum shakes her head, not in the sense that she's agreeing, more as if she doesn't understand what Emily means. Not that bad? The sink's full of dishes! She finds a drinking glass in the cupboard and washes it before filling it with water and drinking from it. She sits down on the sofa and switches the TV off with the remote and asks Emily if there's anything else she needs helping with besides that lamp. Em tells her she's got most things under control, and her mum looks around, looking for something not right, before Emily says, Mum, stop looking for things to criticise.

When Em's mum gets frustrated she puckers her lips and her face goes red. This time (she can't understand what she's done to be spoken to like that) she goes extra red, the colour blotches down her throat, her lips tremble and the water dribbles from the corner of her mouth when she drinks.

When Em's mum gets angry she puckers her lips and for a few seconds thinks unbefitting thoughts a mother shouldn't ever think but which are then gone again in a flash, forgotten about. Because Em's mum, unlike Em herself, and unlike Pablo, is capable of controlling her anger, she puts her anger away in a square box and pushes it to the very back of her mind. She won't retrieve it more than a couple of times a year, when the anger again bubbles up, causing her occasionally to let out something spiteful (once, she threw money at her daughter as if at a dirty whore).

Em's mum was the sort of person who had to do everything herself, who thought that if she put too much chocolate spread on Em's bread the child welfare services would come and take Em away from her.

She's the sort, too, who puts the frighteners on Em and says that if Em gives too much away to the family centre or the health visitor or the midwife, if she says anything at all, the child welfare services can use it against her at some future point in time.

When Em climbs onto the chair to change the light bulb, her mum grips the chair by the legs, she holds it as tight as she can, on all fours, and Em looks down at her back. As she holds, she tells Em about a programme on TV where a woman visits a maternity ward. The small and narrow back of Emily's mum, the line of her knobbly spine. If Em falls, she thinks, she'll use her mum to break her fall, and her mum will break something and be unable to get up.

Em's mum thinks there's a lot that could be criticised, a lot of disorderliness that a person doesn't notice in their own home, which others do notice, like the chairs being different, scratches on the wooden flooring, the cupboards in the kitchen not having been washed, the windows not having been cleaned, greasy marks and dirt showing up when the sun shines through into the flat. After they've eaten (bread rolls her mum brought in a bag), Emily goes into the living room and switches the TV on again and lies down on the sofa. Em's mum sometimes wonders if Em's depressed and can't look after herself anymore, she looks worn out, her face has become pudgy, her hair, gathered in a ponytail, looks greasy. But Emily, everything's such a mess in here, she says, can't you see? Em doesn't answer. Em's lying on the sofa with a woolly blanket over her.

Em's mum says, You need to keep things tidy. She says, You need to get your life together. It's exactly like Em's a teenager again. Her mum makes them a gratin for dinner, says into thin air in the empty kitchen, Why can't you hang a calendar up at least? Then puts the meal out on the table when it's ready, calls for Em, and dishes up for them both. Em doesn't appear for a few minutes (her mum feels like shouting, but you can't do that in such a small flat, what would people think), and when Em does appear she looks at the food and prods at it for quite a while, Sausage gratin, she says, This isn't sausage gratin.

Emily's mum and Emily had lived together all Em's life in the little flat a bit further away in the south of the city, and Emily had been a great kid nearly all her childhood and youth. For a long time they slept together in Em's mum's room, because Emily didn't want to sleep on her own, Emily would wet herself if she slept in her own room and afterwards she'd be ashamed and would hide her knickers in various places around the flat. Once when Emily's mum had a man staying over and Em had to sleep in her own room, she woke in the middle of the night and got up in the dark and went into her mum's room, and when she saw the man, who said hello and crouched down to greet her (luckily he was wearing under-pants), Emily thought it was her dad who'd come back. So that Emily could feel more independent, her mum ordered a sofa bed from IKEA to make Em's room a bit cosier, she could have pretend tea parties on the sofa during the day and then fold it out at bedtime.

When Emily was older they hardly ever argued, Em did the cooking and slept in at the weekends, her mum would knock on her door and go in, would lean over Emily, who'd be smelling all warm and a bit musty, gorgeous, that's what she was, lying there with her makeup still on, and Em's mum would say then that it was time for Emily to get up. And at some point Emily must have grown up and become an adult, her mum can't remember when, it's not that long ago, but she remembers Emily turning in on herself, all of a sudden she wanted to maintain a distance of sorts, she had boyfriends she kept to herself, all of which meant her mum started phoning her for chats, though often she'd only get through to her voicemail.

Often she only gets through to her voicemail. She's asked Emily to text her if she can't answer the phone: Give me a shout when you see this, she writes then, she's lost count of how many times.

But think positive! What a wonder a baby is! A miracle! We mustn't forget it. A woman who's pregnant shouldn't be dreading giving birth, and when she does give birth she should bend forward over her tummy to see the baby come out and help it on its way. It's fantastic, Emily's mum thinks. She'd done just that with Em, helped her into the world and put her to her breast, she lived on her own by then, the father was long gone, and she'd taken Em home with her and washed and dressed her and breastfed her and done everything all by herself. Emily's mum never wondered if things could have been different, it was all just the way it was. She thinks she remembers going up all the stairs with the baby in her arms, rocking the pram on the balcony, but in actual fact she remembers nothing, because no mother really remembers what it was like. True, she didn't get out much when Em was little, but it's nice seeing so many of their things from before now in Emily's flat, she says to Em, and Em rolls her eyes.

Em's mum wonders if choice of men gets handed down, if Em chose wrongly because her mum chose all the wrong men before. Em's mum had a tendency to go for men who turned out to be weak, she's realised that. Men who couldn't cope with being left. Em's dad had snapped completely and gone all dramatic when her mum one day shoved her beer glass to one side on the table in front of her and put a stop to it all. It's no good, she said, I want you out now before the baby's born. I can't be doing with this anymore, she said, and he started throwing things about then and threatening to do away with them all. He'd stood with a knife pointed against her chest and later on that same night with the knife at his own throat, and after a police response saw Em's dad end up crying on the floor without any clothes on, he had no option but to pack his things, go out the door, and never come back.

Emily's mum says of Emily's dad that there was something not right before that as well, something that was already there, he was different somehow. Normal, I wouldn't know about that, she snorts. He was clueless about a lot of things, she says, and snorts again, like ironing sheets and shirts, or knowing how to wrap a present. You should have seen the presents he wrapped! People who don't know how to wrap a present have been handed too much in life, it's like not knowing how to bake a loaf. Your dad somehow managed to bake a green loaf once, Emily's mum says. He never paid a bill, and wouldn't pay the rent either. Your dad was a good ... driver (she lists things he liked and was good at), but I doubt he'd have made a good father.

Emily's mum is three months into the relationship when she first suspects Emily's dad might have a dependency problem. She stands and listens in the hall when he goes into the bedroom and gets his bottle out, unscrews the lid, and gulps down a few mouthfuls. Before he comes out again she's already pretending to be looking for something in her bag, My keys, she says, and he steps past her into the living room where he sits down on the sofa. She'd thought he was chronically fatigued, and once, though only the once, there'd been a funny smell in the bathroom, strong and pungent, and she'd found a lighter on the floor under the sink.

She could still smell it afterwards.

Preferably, she'd have had a man who was a bit dull. Emily's mum can think about it for hours, but it's only a thought, she feels herself grow heavy and warm in her body, a man who goes to work every day, who comes home in the afternoon and is happy with a simple supper, a man who can fix things, shelves and lamps, who can build a bed for a child, a man who'll slip away into a room after his meal and switch the computer on there, to organise something or read the news while she knits.

It happens that she makes herself up, she's looked in Em's drawers, there's lots of different eye shadows there, and lipsticks, she picks the darkest one and runs it once over her lower lip before pinching her lips together. One time when she's got lipstick on, Em says, with what her mum perceives to be disgust, What have you done to yourself, Mum?

When Emily's mum tries to think back on her own time as mother to a small child, she remembers almost nothing, nearly the whole of Em's childhood is a blank to her now, but whether it's because she hardly ever slept or because she's deleted her time with Em's dad from her mind, she has no idea. She can wonder sometimes if she was suffering from postnatal depression. It's difficult to think about.

Thinking back into the past, looking at photos, for instance, makes Emily's mum feel ill at ease, she can hardly swallow and her breathing becomes laboured. Even a little thing like her hair being short and dark twenty years ago, whereas now it's long and mousy, can be enough.

When Emily thinks back on her childhood, she thinks of it as happy, even if all she remembers are glimpses.

She's never known her father, he is, and will remain, a peripheral figure in her life. She knows what her mum's told her, and she knows she looks like him, her wrists, for example, because she doesn't look like her mum, her mum has these terribly thin wrists that she can get her thumb and index finger around. When she was still little Em lied and said her dad was away working in Drammen, and she pictured him working in a chocolate spread factory like the dad of someone in her class did, and when later she met him, once in town, she was so disappointed to find he was short and horrible-looking and worked in an office. Maybe it was because he was so short and horrible-looking that she felt uncomfortable, frightened even, and never wanted to see him again.

Just to think, now she's having a baby and he doesn't even know.

To begin with the neighbour wanted to help her, as a friend, he thought she could do with some help because he hadn't seen the boyfriend in a long time, at least he assumed that was what he was. But why should a person need help just because they're on their own with a swollen tummy? Can the other people in the flats, in the supermarket, tell that she's on her own? Does it show?

The neighbour needs to pull himself together now, stop being so inept and pitiful and nervous.

People like that, who aren't any use, are so annoying.

He can't remember the first time he saw Emily, and feels at once rather sad, no, not sad, wistful, because wouldn't that be something you were supposed to remember?

He's seen her lots of times, in various places, and whenever he sees her he thinks she's really nice (a feeling of joy in every strand of hair).

Once, before he knew her, Em was hardly even pregnant then, at least not enough for anyone to be able to tell, it was a gorgeous day in summer, the neighbour had seen her get rid of a lamp at the entrance to the woods behind the flats (these godawful Soviet-looking blocks, the way they're just there, all upright and blocky). She looked like she was half baked, was dressed all in black, but pretty as well. (Some people from the flats dump all sorts of things at the entrance to the woods, like sofas and mattresses, bin liners full of plastic, bin liners torn apart by crows and magpies, the contents then strewn all over.) He was gathering rubbish up off the lawns, and when she saw him, and saw what he was doing, she almost hadn't the heart anymore to get rid of her lamp, he could tell. On another occasion he'd passed comment when she'd had two wicker chairs with her in the lift, two wicker chairs, nice and worn, like the ones his grandmother used to have in the garden, but that can't have been the first time he saw her either. Is it all right for a person to have a thing about someone they've never really spoken to, he wonders. Now and then he feels an urge to take her by the arm and pull her into his flat when she goes past on the stairs, because maybe she's showing herself off to him, maybe she has a fairly good idea that he's standing there listening behind his door (he imagines she keeps looking at his door). But if he sees her when he's parking the car, she'll lower her eyes straight away and look at the ground or her phone, maybe it's because she's shy and doesn't want him to see that she's blushing, maybe she doesn't know what to say, and neither does he.

He's put a new name on his door, a big white oblong of folded A4, with his name on it: Jan Smith-Andreassen. (After a period of much consideration he's decided to change his name by adding a hyphen to Smith Andreassen. Not the most drastic alteration, you might think, but he thinks that in this way he's honouring his mother and father at the same time.) He's standing now behind the door, inside his flat, listening. It's rather an old door, one that swings shut on its own, and flimsy too, you can hear whenever anyone's on the stairs, and so he often stands and listens when someone's going up or coming down, and if that person happens to be stepping very lightly he knows it's the young woman who's pregnant. He's not actually a stalker, to begin with he simply got up from his chair every now and then to keep tabs on the downstairs neighbours where young men are always going in and out, and sometimes when he steps onto his balcony he can smell marijuana. She's coming now. On her way down, gripping the handrail, she glances at his door.

She sees his new name sign on the door and can't remember what it said before, was he living with someone and isn't anymore, or wasn't there one? Em pauses a moment and gazes at the door, then carries on cautiously down the stairs.

Is the neighbour a pastor? She thinks he is, but do pastors look like that? She doesn't know what pastors are like, but she assumes they must be very nice. Or is he something else, a social worker maybe, or a tram driver, who knows, she likes going on the metro and the trams, but oh, what an awfully lonely job that must be, all on your own in the driver's cab at the front, pulling into and away from the platforms all day long. And in actual fact, he's always been fond of railway systems and public transport, he can find himself thinking about the new tram line that's to run alongside Ring 2, or the metro line that's going to go to Fornebu, and he can get quite excited, so that his hands tremble almost.

No, she thinks he's a pastor, because she's seen periodicals left on his doormat with the word Parish on them.

She wonders: Does he think things like God sees into his heart??

She wonders: Does he sometimes feel that it's basically only before God that one can be human???

The neighbour, you can tell just by looking at him, you can see by the way he walks, the clothes he wears, those worn-out blue jeans with the seams coming apart at the crotch because his thighs keep rubbing against each other all the time, you can tell he needs something in his life.

He always says hello in the lift, but never more than that, usually he'll just stare into space without ever looking at her, waiting for the lift to reach the third floor where he'll then step out. When Pablo was still here, it's a while ago now, the neighbour would just acknowledge them with a nod or else would say something about the weather, a bit nippy out, something like that. Pablo never said anything (Pablo doesn't know how to talk to strangers). What does the neighbour think concerning Pablo? Didn't he realise that Emily was with-with Pablo? Hasn't he got any morals?

It's not his fault he's a poor soul. Now he's sent her a note, put it in her letter box. She finds it in with all the junk mail: Hope you've had a nice day.

That Friday he opens his door, Hi, he says, with a wave or perhaps just a lift of his hand, and Em says hi back, softly, just as she's breathing out, because she's going down the stairs, going rather quickly for someone so big, and she isn't holding the handrail like she ought to. He doesn't come after her but drops a pair of wet trainers onto his doormat and shuts the door again. And inside his cramped one-bedroom flat on the outskirts of Oslo he stands and wonders why he wrote that note. His heart thumps because of that stupid note.

The neighbour's a simple soul, or rather NO, HE ISN'T, but he is in a way, like when you say that something boring is negative, whereas something normal is positive, if that makes any sense. Okay, it doesn't, but the point is that he's not that good at being bored. The neighbour is the sort of person who's only got one pair of jeans and when they get worn out he buys another pair exactly the same. In the afternoons and evenings he plays on his PlayStation and listens to music, watches some TV, prepares for the following day at work, whatever it is he does, he brushes up on what he's going to say, and practises saying it out loud. And every night before he goes to bed he makes himself a packed lunch, four slices of rye bread, two with liver paste and two with ham and mayonnaise. He puts sandwich paper between them and wraps them up, puts the parcel in a plastic bag, and opens the fridge.

There's a lot that has to be sorted before he can feel at ease, he needs clean floors, a tidy worktop in the kitchen, properly stacked books, the neighbours' doormats have got to be straight, the landings mustn't be cluttered with footwear and umbrellas. One day the Somali family have moved one of their leather sofas out onto the landing, it stays there for weeks. Their kids sit there and play games on their phones, instead of inside. He hears loud voices, he hears doors slamming, and it's early evening when he sits down and writes a note on a yellow PostIt he sticks on the family's door: Hi, your sofa's in the way out here. It's a fire hazard. Can we do something about it? Yours, THE COMMITTEE.

He goes to bed, his hands on top of the duvet, arms at his sides then under the duvet where it's warm, and before he goes to sleep he turns onto his side. Before he goes to sleep he thinks about Emily, about Emily's breasts, about Emily's swollen tummy, no, he thinks about his mother and how she used to sit beside his bed and soothe him to sleep, her hands smoothing his cheek, his hair, how she made his packed lunches for him, every morning there'd be a packed lunch put out for him, a parcel of white greaseproof paper with the ends tucked in, until suddenly she was making his packed lunches with stale bread. Only a few months passed then before his mother was so confused she couldn't keep the place clean anymore either, everything was a mess, dirty and foul-smelling.

He sees in his mind's eye his mother's kitchen just after she died, an unimaginable clutter, filth and mould, and a very particular smell he hasn't ever managed to put into words, he pictures his mother and can smell the alarm clock that used to be hers, and realises there's a musty smell in the room from poor air circulation.

He'll fall asleep in a moment now, the neighbour, just a few more thoughts remain. He wonders if he's got a problem, and of course he has. Every now and then he feels like an empty coke bottle, with only a few watery drops left at the bottom, that someone surely will give a kick and send spinning across the tarmac. Has he actually got a thing about her, or is he just looking for some sort of human contact? He's not sure.

AT THE POLICE STATION

It's Monday and she's got an appointment at the police station. Ever since late on Wednesday, after she finished work, came home, and opened her letter box to find the letter in a white envelope, she's thought about what she's going to say, what this "voluntary interview" will be like, what they're going to ask her about, what the police station, the rooms inside it, the faces, and the uniforms are going to look like.

The letter, that's now in Emily's bag, says You are advised to attend, it says 1 p.m. and the address she's to go to.

Pablo hardly ever phones now (he phones when he wants), but a few days ago he phoned and said it was cold out and that he'd been walking for a long time, but he didn't say how long he'd been walking or where he was. It was up to him to tell her, not up to her to ask questions, and anyway people were always asking too many questions, he said, and people were being difficult too, not paying him the money he was due, and someone else was a thieving bastard. He'd been crashing at a mate's place where he had his own room, his own bed, and this mate of his had apparently shown him how to make these really good pancakes with eggs and flour and milk and bananas, you mashed the bananas with a fork and it was important the bananas were brown and soft. The pancakes turned out a bit fatter and a bit lumpier, Pablo said, the banana made them sweeter and they were even better with chocolate spread on. He'd gone to sleep and the next day his phone and his mate's phone were both gone, so he was phoning from another phone now. The sun had been nice and warm the day before, not that warm, but warmish, and he'd only been out a couple of hours at the most, and only in the quieter streets, in case the police saw him. Emily doesn't get a word in edgeways when he's on the phone to her, he goes on and on, and eventually she cuts him off and says, Aren't you coming home again, and he says, Not yet, and she says, But I'm pregnant, you can't just disappear, and then he says he's got to hang up.

' Her tummy is big and heavy, she has to move cautiously, she has to hold her hands under her belly, all the other passengers from the metro stride past her, they're in such a hurry and Em wishes she could reach out to them and say wait for me. She's still on the platform when everyone else has got to the escalators.

She has to walk all the way to the police station and it's quite far, she has to cross over a lot of crossings, and then she has to go through a door and up to a desk, where she has to say her name and who she's got an appointment with. Em's planned what she's going to say, she imagines a policeman in uniform who calls her name out from behind the desk, and she gets up then and says her name and that she's been called in for a voluntary interview, and the policeman then leads her to some room or other, down a corridor they walk, and he supports her by the arm.

But no, inside the police station it's a woman behind the desk and she takes her up to the third floor and down a long corridor on the left. Em finds a WC there and sits on the loo for quite some time, to be on her own for a bit, to rest, because her stomach aches, she's been keeping it in for so long. She folds a piece of toilet paper and places it in her knickers, flushes the toilet, washes her hands, and looks at herself in the mirror.

She's given some coffee in a paper cup along with three little plastic pots of cream. She empties all three into the coffee and stirs with her little finger. She doesn't quite know where to begin, the policewoman suggests they can start with the first time she and Pablo met. Do you think you can describe that to me? We're interested in anything at all that might help us gain a picture, the policewoman says.

Em tells her what comes into her mind, her life story in many ways. While she's talking, the policewoman yawns three and a half times (but manages to contain the fourth).

Em had noticed Pablo several times in her life, before they got together, so hadn't she always fancied him, in a way? One time she saw him in the supermarket. She was fifteen. He'd have been seventeen. She didn't know how old he was then, he used to go to the same school as her, only she wasn't sure what year he was in. He was tidying the shelves, straightening the toilet rolls, which is a no-win sort of job, because the toilet-roll packets are so big that as soon as a customer takes one off the shelf it leaves a great big hole and looks disorderly. When Em went to the checkout to pay, Pablo came hurrying over to scan her items, he skipped over a soft-drinks crate that had been left out in the aisle, nimble and quick as lightning, or no, like an athlete. They exchanged glances but didn't speak to each other, apart from him saying how much it was and asking if she wanted the receipt.

Em's seventeen the first time she speaks to Pablo, the first time they talk-talk to each other, on a night out from work, and Pablo places the flat of his hand between her shoulder blades when she gets up so as to stop her from falling. She's been on the beers with the other staff, and she's drunk and speed-talking, she talks so fast she can't keep up and has to leave out the odd word or two. Pablo, who works in a different supermarket, but the same chain, says, Haven't I seen you somewhere before, and Em says, No, I don't think so, and Pablo says, Yes, I have, you used to come into the supermarket where I work, and then Em says, No, that'd be my sister.

Em pictures Pablo the way he was on that night out, white trousers and a white low-neck T-shirt.

Black belt and a black hoodie vest. Pablo may have been short, but he was really cute and caring, really warm with her when he wanted to be warm. (I can't understand what she sees in him, I've no idea how anyone can fall in love with someone like that, his smile takes up too much of his face.)

Sometimes love comes creeping up on you, and sometimes it comes like a bolt of lightning out of the blue, and Em can't tell the two kinds apart. ALL EMILY WANTS IS TO BE LOVED, that's all any young woman wants, isn't it? To be loved for their looks (?) and their youth (?), and later it's probably something else you get loved for, something deeper, only she's not going to get that far. It's as if Emily gets no further in her infatuation, she doesn't know what it means and can't describe it in any other way than that Pablo was a good laugh and cute. Is it like getting stung by a wasp, to begin with it hurts like mad but eventually a little brown mark on your hand is all there is? How are you supposed to describe being infatuated with someone when it's the police questioning you, or not questioning you exactly, because you're just helping them with their inquiries, but how are you supposed to explain that to a matter-of-fact policewoman making matter-of-fact notes in scribbly handwriting in a police notebook?

It was nice, says Em, he was sitting on the sofa looking at me all the time and I was looking at him, and she thought then that it might come to something and it did.

Pablo had gone home with her to hers, up all the stairs and into the little flat, she'd shown him round, this is the hall, this is the loo, this is the kitchen, these are my things, and Pablo had looked and then picked up the glass ornament off the shelf, the little bird, yes, she was fairly certain that was what he'd done, and after that he'd sat down on the sofa. Em had sat down next to him and Pablo then put his arm around her shoulder and it gave her goose bumps all over, from where his hand was touching her, all the way down her back.

Was she pure and innocent then? Until she's spread her legs in a bed and maybe on a playing field, in the middle of the night on a playing field, she's a bit like a sixteen-year-old who doesn't understand how you actually get off with someone, she thinks it's by looking at each other, and then it just happens. It's the same for Pablo, he doesn't know a thing. They don't know a thing, either of them, they go around town, light summer nights, lilacs in the air, Pablo tears the heads off the lilacs and eats them, it's then that he's irresistible to her, she has to think about him all the time. What was it she fell for, that he was a good laugh and cute, yes, that he put his arm around her shoulder and asked if she was okay with that, that his hand touched her, was he stroking her with that hand, was that how he touched her, or was it just resting? She can't remember. Her heart pounded (Pablo's heart pounded too), it was the first time in Emily's life she'd done anything like it. More happens after that. Em says that she and Pablo had sex a lot of times, several times a day, is she supposed to go into detail, tell them how Pablo liked to have sex with her on the balcony, Em's forehead pressed against the glass, that she had to wipe away the greasy marks afterwards?

Pablo sends her texts, Em's got her phone folded and when she opens it a big yellow envelope appears on the screen. Wassup, Pablo texts. And then, What you doin? Are you in? Are you in? Can I come over?

And later Pablo says to her they'll stick together here for a few years, then relocate, relocate to Costa Rica, it's a great place, or no, back to Santiago, they'll buy a car, a new car, and they'll have a kid, then another kid, and the kids can be with his family, you won't even have to work. You won't miss any of this, says Pablo.

Her stomach was in turmoil after that.

The police think Em knows something about Pablo and what they found in the flat, only Em doesn't know why they're asking her, why they called her in, why they're questioning her when she doesn't know anything of any significance. She really doesn't know anything. She imagines herself knowing more, that when Pablo pulls wads of money out of his pocket she knows where it comes from, whose hands have been on it, who talks to who. She imagines herself buying heroin, but she doesn't even know what heroin is, and that she gives the money to Ousman, under some stairs, under the stairs in her building.

Pablo made Em feel like a celeb (?), she'd felt pretty, he'd given her a butterfly necklace, and if she came walking along the street, towards Pablo, to where he was sitting at a table, Pablo would whistle at her. Is that what she thinks, that big stars are perfect and always on the front foot? Pablo ruined Em's sleep and her eating habits too, she got thinner. Once, Pablo had taken her to a proper place with white tablecloths and nice glasses, he told Em she could have whatever she wanted. Whatever I want? Em said, and could see that everything was really expensive, and Pablo nodded. Anything for you, he even said. So Em had starters as well as a main course, and two glasses of wine, she remembers it even if she doesn't say so, and although she hadn't ordered a dessert, Pablo was furious when he saw the bill, he said they ought to do a runner, he kept going over the bill for mistakes and refused to leave a tip.

Em thinks about Pablo's face, the mole on his cheek, his yellow hue. It hurts, it hurts inside her head when Em thinks of Pablo dumping her. Isn't that what he's done?

She could have said something about Pablos' body, that he's, no, was thin and wiry, that there was a sheen to his forehead, while other times he was completely dry. Em thought his body must be like a raisin, because she'd never seen him drink water. Pablo would often drink coffee, preferably a whole pot, four or five cups one after another, or several cups of instant, several cups of coffee from the coffee machine in the REMA supermarket, but he rarely drank water. He never drank water after they'd had sex and he never drank water when he woke up, not even after a night with a lot of Jack Daniel's did he ever drink water.

Em doesn't tell the policewoman everything she knows, though the policewoman does all she can to get inside Em's innermost thoughts and feelings.

Had Em ever met Pablo's family, Pablo's sister, no, she hadn't, only the sister, and one time she'd seen

Pablo's mum getting into a car, another time she'd seen his mum on the balcony smoking a cigarette, and when she was finished she flicked the cigarette end out onto the pavement. And another time someone tossed an empty beer can onto the pavement (the pavement below the balcony, cigarette ends everywhere). Everyone said Pablo's mum was old, a bit of a head case, mental, that she was claiming disability benefit when there was nothing wrong with her. Mum's ill, said Pablo, and Em imagined Pablo's mother lying in bed, in a room with dark, heavy curtains. Stuffy air, his sleeping mother woken up by her kids every now and then so they could get some food inside her. She'd be lifted out of her bed to go to the toilet, Pablo carries her over to a loo on wheels that can be moved about and emptied like an old-fashioned pot. And Pablo's grandmother was deaf and blind, she'd be sitting on the sofa in a leopard-print loungewear set and his uncles' dogs would be jumping up and walking across her lap. Who are you, the grandmother asks, and Em says, I'm Stefan's daughter, and the grandmother would wonder then if there was a Stefan there too, but no, Em's come on her own to see her. She'd hold Em's face in her hands, her soft wrinkly hands would feel about and explore Emily's face while her throaty voice murmured regrets, alas and alack, about what, about life, and the uncles would heat up some sort of soup in the microwave and fill a sippy cup with it and give it to the grandmother to drink.

In the space of the hour it takes most people to do something, Pablo would do three things, Em tells the policewoman. Pablo was very efficient. In what way, the policewoman wants to know. I don't know, says Em. He did lots of things all at once. And he kept lots of stuff. A lot of old phones and thingamajigs. Pablo invented a receptacle for used snus. He thought there should be something like an ashtray for when people needed to dispose of the soggy little sachets after sucking all the nicotine from the tobacco in them. Two pubs had bought two of Pablo's receptacles, Em says. The policewoman asks what pubs. A sports pub was one, that's all I can remember, says Em. And the policewoman writes all this down in her notebook. (Her writing gets wonkier and wonkier as she goes along.)

It's the policewoman's face, her flat pancake face, that makes Em lose the thread, she can't remember what she was going to say now. The policewoman with her high eyebrows, her hair gathered in a tight knot at the nape (don't they always look like that?), the policewoman, the way she talks through such a little mouth, the way her spit builds up inside her mouth, Em can hear her spit as she speaks, the way she keeps spelling things out to Em, making things clear, saying some things twice. The policewoman extends a clean white hand that's both soft and firm, and Em pictures her browsing in furniture stores and buying vases. Those stripy vases that are white and silver, or vases made out of blue glass.

And then the policewoman puts her hand down flat on the table and says it's time for a break, she gets up and leaves the room. In the break room several of her colleagues are sitting drinking coffee, they've got some chocolates in a bowl as well and someone offers her one. How are you getting on, a male colleague asks, Making inroads? And the policewoman shakes her head and swears in frustration, because the pregnant Emily's saying nothing at all that's relevant. Lean on her, the man says, lean on her a bit, he repeats, she's got to know something. But she's so young, the policewoman says, she doesn't know anything, she's like twenty years old.

The policewoman, who likes to categorise people and assign them to different levels, even though levels isn't a word you can use about people, thinks that Emily is the way she is because she wasn't very good at school, not that she was trouble, but because she was too far away, because there was so much going on in the classroom that took away Emily's attention. There was a girl like her in every class, the policewoman thought, girls with that empty blank dreamy veil of a look in their eyes. Water bottles with slices of lemon in them, an earphone stuck in one ear, girls who never get started on the exercise the teacher hands out, and it's girls like that who end up working on the checkout in KIWI. Not that Emily's stupid, she's just not very smart, the policewoman thinks, Emily's perhaps level two.

The policewoman comes back with a mug of coffee for herself and one in a paper cup for Em. Now she wants to know what Pablo does for a living, where he gets his money from, and Em puts her head in her hands for the fifth time and says she doesn't know what he does, and so the policewoman asks Em again and asks Em again and again. Pablo did jobs for his mates, deliveries, that kind of thing, Em says. One time he went out in the evening to give someone a hand shifting some stuff and when he came home in the early morning he said he'd been filling in on a night shift. I haven't a clue, Em says. The money was in the car, in the compartment between the front seats. You mean under the dashboard, the policewoman says, writing it all down in her notebook. No, in that compartment by the gear lever, says Em. Pablo opened it and there it was, all in big notes. So he kept money lying about like that in the car, the policewoman says. In that compartment, the key compartment or whatever it's called, Em says. Yes, I've got that, the policewoman says with some annoyance. Now she wants to ask Em about something a bit delicate.

She wants to know if Em's ever been subjected to violence, but what sort of violence, proper violence or just slap-in-the-face sort of violence, or is that violence as well?

Once, she'd been dragged by the hair down several of the seven flights of stairs (the lift's often stuck, therefore the stairs), but it was only the once and had never happened again, and afterwards Pablo had been seized with shame and guilt, he'd only done it because Em had headbutted him. Does she tell the policewoman this too? Why she'd head-butted him is something Em can't remember. After it happened she stood in front of the mirror in the bathroom pulling out tufts of her hair (now she's a battered little flower poking up meekly from the soil), and one of the old ladies from the block always smiled at her after that, a sad and pitying smile, whenever she saw Emily on the lawns, among the trees. Had the old lady seen what happened? Had she heard what had been going on?

Most likely it was something Em had said that made Pablo grab her by the arm, his fingers had dug into her upper arm, and Em had smacked her fore-head into his face in return, causing Pablo to stagger and fall, and Em had run to the lift and pressed the button repeatedly, but then he got hold of her by the hair. Em recounts what happened in part, but only in part. The policewoman says that men who've been violent will be violent again, even if they've only been violent the once, and Em tries to tell her that she was the one who'd started it, being violent to him, Pablo had only defended himself.

The policewoman says it's normal to think like that when you're a victim and that Em should try and start thinking about a life without Pablo. Step away, if only gradually, stand on your own two feet, the sun's not going to shine tomorrow, but in time it will. Think about the baby, the policewoman says with a nod towards Em's tummy.

Anyway, Pablo never actually lived with her in the flat, not really, it was more on and off, he'd stay the night, kept a few things there, IKEA bags shoved under the bed, Em cleared a drawer for him to put his clothes in, but he only used it for his bits and bobs, his chargers and keys, lighters and condoms. And Pablo slept well into the mornings, like it was a hotel, he could eat four eggs for breakfast and would fry Em a couple too, and two eggs on a plate made her feel like she was being looked after.

The police have gathered some more information.

Pablo had been seeing other girls (without Emily knowing), beautiful young girls with the smoothest skin, the smoothest brows, and had told them they'd got nothing to be afraid of, Pablo wasn't dangerous, he was a nice person.

Without Emily knowing, Pablo had been chatting other girls up, coming on to other girls, standing next to other girls, drawing himself up to his full height, breathing into their faces and saying, Do you work in the creative industries too?

He'd been sending notes to other girls, inviting them to various parties or outlining his latest invention.

The police knew all this because they'd spoken to two of the girls who'd turned up in reception the morning after the photo of Pablo appeared in the newspapers. Or no, that wasn't it, it wasn't a photo in the newspapers, it was the police hanging around outside Pablo's flat looking for information, standing outside asking whoever came out of the building if they'd seen this man (photo of Pablo and Ousman and so on). Pablo hadn't struck anyone as a bad-boy type, more as someone a bit clueless, a bit stupid perhaps. The girls approached the male police officer, they thought he looked good in his uniform. He talked to them while looking pleased with himself, the policewoman took down what they said and asked if Pablo had been carrying a holdall with him, but the girls couldn't remember. Did Pablo come across like he'd taken drugs? The girls couldn't say. Was there anything else about Pablo they'd noticed? The answer was a definite no.

Pablo sounds, how to put it, a bit deficient, maybe, he's not all there, is what the policewoman thought.

Two more pieces of information have come in.

The first came from some former schoolmates (five in all, who'd "broken out" of the environment they'd grown up in), they'd heard Pablo was selling weed down the precinct, they'd heard Pablo had progressed to selling weapons, they'd heard too that Pablo had started working as a nightclub bouncer. How anyone could be selling weapons from a small flat without getting copped, the policewoman has no idea, because that sort of thing is something the police have got pretty much under control and neither she nor anyone else at the station has heard anything about it before now. The five former schoolmates talked about this as if it was common knowledge, one of them for instance had been at someone's flat where they kept weapons in a big plastic storage box under the bed. Poor Emily, they all said, the five who were tipping the police off, it's a wonder she sticks with him.

The second piece of information came from a female drug addict who claimed she'd had sex with Pablo and that Pablo had robbed her. She came into the police station shouting her head off almost, I'VE GOT SOME INFORMATION! The woman's hair was gathered in a tight ponytail, she had a coat on, and a pair of sunglasses, lip gloss.

Pablo wore baggy pants, hoodies, sunglasses, and had a wispy beard in the middle of his chin, said the woman.

She'd met Pablo in a bar across from REMA, the one by the car park. Pablo had been staring at her all night and she'd got talking to him, had a few beers with him, Pablo drank five beers and she drank four, and eventually she went with him into one of the brown blocks of flats, to what he told her was his own flat. And there was a mate of Pablo's there who gave a scornful laugh and then fetched a big glass of orange juice from the kitchen. She took her clothes off, Pablo pulled her knickers down, took his trousers off and his boxers, and then the drug addict woman told him he had to use a condom, to which Pablo said, Very funny. Afterwards the drug addict woman passed out and when she came round her phone was gone, her wallet was gone, and her earphones were gone. Her jacket was gone too. Pablo wasn't in the flat and when she knocked on the door of his mate's room he flew off the handle and started shouting at her, told her to get lost, started shoving her, threatening her, told her to get lost and flung her shoes out onto the stairs.

The policewoman asked if either of them had hit her, she just wanted to know if there was anything to be taken down, whether she wanted to report anyone for assault, and the drug addict woman snorted then and said, There's no point telling you, you haven't got a clue what I'm talking about.

A few days later the police speak to Pablo's mate Danny (the police aren't sure where he's from, or originally from, South America or Southeast Asia). The police ask him if he knows anything about this blah blah blah this drugged-up woman who passed out, does he know anything about the flat, for example, or about Ousman the Pakistani (short and fattish, but underneath it all just a quiet lad who never quite got things together, like what, well, like school, a regular job, that sort of thing), and Danny gives a shrug as if he knows nothing, and the police ask if Danny knows about anyone else being involved, like Pablo for instance, they've heard some rumours going round, for instance that Pablo's girlfriend's nearly nine months gone. But you'll know that already, you'll have met her, they say, and hasn't Pablo gone off and left her in the lurch, his pregnant girlfriend, what do you think about that? Pablo's on the level, he's just had a run of bad luck that's all, says Danny, like with that girlfriend of his, it's no secret. We talk to you lot all the time, you know that, I can sit here as long as you want me to, he says.

Afterwards Danny sends Pablo a text: Hahaha, it says.

WORK, MONEY, AND HEALTH

When she's on the early shift she has to be in the shop by half past five, open up, turn the lights on, switch the cash registers on, restock the bread and milk, the baked goods need to be set out, and other goods too. It's always Marewan who's on early with her, because it's Marewan himself who draws up the rosters. He must think I'm good at my job, Emily thinks. And in fact she is quite good at smiling and being service-minded.

At three minutes to six, Em and Marewan unlock the door and the customers can come in. The first customers buy only baked goods and energy drinks, a lot buy snus and cigarettes too. By nine the first of the beer customers turn up. After that it's the lunch crowd, and baked goods again. Marewan spends a whole half-hour in the toilets, Em can sit in peace and do her nails (she's never got dirty fingernails even though in a way she's quite poor), a very calming activity, she finds.

A bit later she has to sort the vegetables, make sure the fruit's still fresh, fetch a basket, fill the basket with the apples that have got brown marks on them, take the basket into the back room and put it with the rest of the waste items that need to go out. Em takes two lots of strawberries for tasters, washes them and fills them into two bowls she puts out among the rest of the fruit and veg. Marewan rings the bell and she goes back to the checkout, enters in the customer's items, asks them if they want a bag, the receipt, no, no bag, presses Void Item, and the customer (man, sixtyish) then stands and gives her a now-you're-for-it sort of look and closely, closely checks his receipt.

She mustn't forget that the health centre (the family centre, the family welfare office, the family helpline?) is supposed to phone her on Wednesday. Weren't they supposed to phone? Or was she supposed to phone them?

The neighbour, or the pastor, comes into the supermarket today as well, he lingers for a long time at the bread rolls and small cakes without buying any of them. Usually he'll buy a loaf and a packet of sliced processed meat and some tinned meatballs. He can buy the same thing several times in a row and then not turn up again for weeks on end. As if all he eats is tinned meatballs and nothing else (he shops elsewhere as well, because the supermarket where Em works is often disorderly, with long queues at the checkout, only she doesn't know this). Today he buys toilet paper, washing-up liquid, juice, coffee, a packet of sliced processed meat, and a loaf of bread. He stands there with two hundred-krone notes at the ready, and when Em enters in his items, her mouth closes all of a sudden by itself, as if she's unsettled by him, and she can't say anything. Drool comes out of her mouth instead of words (bag? receipt?) and not being able to ask she enters in a bag too, it doesn't cost much, she perhaps thinks, though probably it's just force of habit, she enters one in without thinking. She sends the bag off down the conveyor, before he's paid, he's standing in front of her ready to pay, money in hand, and then he asks Em if she can cancel the bag. He asks her nicely, he's not stroppy about it. He just says he didn't want a bag, that he'd rather not walk around advertising such a big capitalist concern. It's like walking around with a sandwich board, the pastor says. Without either of us gaining from it, only the company.

On another occasion he told her she was smiling like the sun the way she was sitting there. Was that a compliment or something more intimidating?

What's going to happen with the baby, are you going to have it all on your own, have you got enough money, you'll be needing more money won't you, you won't have enough, what if you run out, how am I going to help you then, Emily's mum wants to ask, only she doesn't know how, and for that reason she keeps quiet.

She comes into the flat, takes over the flat, her smell, her things everywhere. Emily's mum's brought a trolley case with her, she puts it next to the sofa, and inside it her clothes have been folded in neat rectangles and tucked into plastic bags. Emily's mum spends a whole day buying new things for the flat. Bowls and pillows and dishcloths, Christmas decorations and feeding bottles, and miscellaneous baby items. She's got her own key now, so she can come and go. The baby'll be here soon, it's best for you not to be on your own, her mum says as Em comes out from the bathroom. When I had you, I wasn't settled either, I had a tatty old sofa someone had given me. I can sleep on yours while I'm here, she says. Probably it's meant to be a comfort on the part of Emily's mum. Emily's mum does the dusting and cleans the bathroom, she sprays blue window cleaner on the mirror and wipes it away with a tea towel, she puts Em's things out, lines them up in rows on the table in the living room. Em lies on the sofa and her mum points at each of her things in turn. Is this to be kept? What's this for? Do you really need two? Most of the things are binned into a big black bin bag, the rest go back on the shelf in the bathroom. Em's accumulated a lot of strange clutter this past couple of years, things she's left and forgotten, used-up lotions, elastic bands, bars of soap, hair clips, things her mum calls junk, things her mum says the baby can harm itself on, even though it'll be a while yet before the child can walk, and Em finds it hard to just get rid of it all. Now her mum's tidied and cleaned her way through the entire flat, the place smells of detergent, and the last of the shampoo bottles goes away under the sink. There we are, she says. Now you need to think about where the cot's going to go. A baby doesn't need much the first year or so, but it does need a cot.

But hasn't she got a job to go to? How come she's here all the time?

Up until two years ago, Em's mum worked in a playgroup, in the creche with the youngest. She was the sort of play assistant who worried a lot, and not just on the inside, she'd be a visible bag of nerves by the time the parents came to pick up their kids.

After a good many years outdoors, in red or blue overalls, Emily's mum lost her balance up by the swings, she fell on the hard, slippery snow and broke her shoulder.

Not good, the playgroup leader said when Emily's mum had to go on the sick for weeks and then months. And when she had to undergo surgery on her shoulder, after a long time in pain, the playgroup leader said the same thing again, and from there it wasn't far to the dole, and later, when she'd become a completely unemployable person, to disability benefit.

Em's mum says something one day about the weather, and after that she says something about someone she bumped into down at the crossroads. Then she says, sternly, trying to be firm, that Em should eat up her breakfast. She tries to make it sound funny too, she thinks, the way she would say things to Em when Em was a child, but Em glares at her nonetheless, before erupting, FOR GOD'S SAKE, CAN'T YOU JUST, after which she spits some yoghurt back into her bowl and locks herself in the bathroom. It's a while before her mum gets to her feet, her hands are trembling, before she picks up the bowl of yoghurt and holds it under the tap, she washes up the coffee cups, too, and the frying pan. Oh no, she's upset now! She's never been spoken to like that before in her life (so she thinks), how can a daughter behave in such a way, all she wanted was to help, she can't understand it. She thinks about Em when Em was still in her early teens, Em at sixteen, refusing to come home, Em standing outside the flats swearing up at her, or when Em got it into her head she was going to move to another city, or another country, to Santiago, she can't quite remember where it was, and anyway she's not sure if Santiago's a city or a country, but she'd said to her then, But what on earth for, she couldn't understand, it frightened her, and Em had said, Because I want to, I want to move away, I'm grown up now, you can't interfere in my life anymore. She didn't know what to do then and got three hundred kroner in notes out of her purse and threw them in Em's face when they were meant to be having a nice birthday meal out at a restaurant. Em's mum can't understand why her daughter is so externalising in her behaviour or why she sees Em coming apart at some point, losing hold of herself, Em climbing up onto a stool on the balcony and tipping herself over the railing.

It shouldn't be forgotten though, that there are two or three songs that can always get Emily's mum back into the swing of things again, that can make her straighten up and look on the bright side (?), see a ray of hope (?) or even a future (??), songs that give her a lift, a gentle nudge in the right direction. There's that one by Lisa Ekdahl, and one by Veronica Maggio, they're playing it on the radio now as she does the dishes, the cups and the knives and forks, the plates (which Em hasn't rinsed, bits of crispbread now stuck). At times like this moment, washing up's all right.

On Saturday mornings she gets up early and takes the metro into town to her spinning at the fitness centre in the Oslo Spektrum building. She scans her membership card and goes into the changing rooms, locks her bag away in a locker and goes into the spinning room, gets on the bike, a lot of women go there, all so they can get something out of their system, a rage of some kind maybe, or just an uptightness. It's not often any of them listen to music anymore, apart from when they're doing the cooking, or in the car, they definitely don't listen to music actively, and definitely not as loud as in the spinning room. They reach their arms into the air, cautiously, stretching the muscles in their backs, and after a while, when their bodies are warm and soft, they're guided by the instructor through a landscape of gentle and harder climbs, faster flat terrain and agreeable descents, the instructor yells at them to up the tempo, and the women (nearly all women) pedal as fast as they can, and at the end they flap their hands in front of their faces or even punch the air.

She's also been wanting to feel her daughter's tummy. One day, without warning, without asking, she reaches a hand out and does.

Em's mum feels Em's tummy, Em doesn't pull away, she doesn't move her mum's hand away but sits there calmly, maybe even leans back a bit into the sofa, while her mother strokes her tummy and waits for the baby to react. Em's mum, who hasn't touched a pregnant tummy since she was pregnant herself, it'll be twenty years ago now, is surprised to find it not to be soft at all, but rather hard. Em's mum, who needed such a long time to pluck up the courage for this that she only feels Em's tummy the once before the baby arrives.

Before the health visitor comes, Em's mum goes back and forth between the living-room table and the kitchen worktop. She puts out a few things, some wafer biscuits, two rolls from the baker's that she halves and puts on a plate. She says something as she busies about: It's very important that Em doesn't tell them anything concrete (and they must be calm and show them this is a good place for a child to grow up), if she tells them anything concrete, they might want to take the baby away from her, it could mean they decide to place the baby in an institution to monitor its development more closely, at worst it could mean them placing the baby in foster care.

The health visitor has a look round the flat before sitting down and producing a number of leaflets and a notepad. She puts the leaflets on the table so that Em and her mum can look at them. The leaflets say, Welcome to the district, What to pack in your natal bag, If you need someone to talk to, What if your baby won't stop crying. The important things, the health visitor says, are not to shake the baby if you're angry, and breastfeeding, the baby will want your breast from the start. She's brought a knitted ball with her that's meant to be a breast and shows Em how the baby will latch on to the nipple. Em's mum mentions baby formula and the health visitor say it usually isn't necessary, but by all means, if needs be, and Em's mum explains that Em didn't want the breast when she was a baby, Em became thin thin, and her mum had to give her a bottle.

I was on my own with her too, Em's mum says. Her father was never in the picture. I understand, says the health visitor. He never paid any maintenance either, Em's mum says, But everything's going to be just fine, she adds, I'm here too. Having such a strong mother will be good for her, the health visitor says, as if Em wasn't there, and then she moves on to the wider situation with Pablo. Have you spoken to the father? she asks. No, we don't talk, says Em, He won't answer his phone.

Normally, we say it's important for the father to sign the acknowledgement of paternity before the birth, but it can be done at the hospital as well, the health visitor says, Has he said anything in the way of not wanting children, anything like that? Em doesn't know how to answer that, she says that Pablo had been intending to come to the meeting where they'd agreed he would sign the acknowledgement of paternity.

For many children, feeling connected with a father is important (it can be harder for a boy to grow up without a father than for a girl), the health visitor says, completely as if she's forgotten what Em's mum just said. Are there any other father figures in the family that could play a role? the health visitor asks. No, says Em. Well, I do have a brother, says Em's mum, and the health visitor says they can get together and have a word about it nearer the time. She writes it down on her notepad and hasn't touched her coffee yet, although she has drunk a whole glass of water.

After the health visitor has gone, Em's mum puts the things in the dishwasher and switches it on. She runs a cloth over the table and tries to say something reasonable about the situation and that everything's going to work out just fine. Em's already turned the TV on. Her mum moves over to the sofa too, she puts Em's feet in her lap and gives them a rub. Perhaps she asks Em if she's thought about whether she wants her to stay after the baby comes, because this is what Em's mum is wondering, and Em says of course she wants her to stay, which basically means that she can see how things might pan out otherwise.

Some people just have to make do with what they had before, the way Em's mum did when she threw Em's dad out, the way Em's nan made do without Em's grandad, the way Em's doing now, the way women usually do, because you don't know what you've got and what you haven't until you clap eyes on something else. And when Em this Wednesday morning claps eyes on Harry and Meghan's wedding on TV, she finds herself thinking about some big questions she's never thought about before: Is that actually a thing you can get, a princess's wedding? Are there really people who live like that? Harry gets up before Meghan every single day so he can make her a cup of cardamom tea with milk in. And Harry says Meghan's his bestie. And Meghan's wearing a long white dress and Harry gives a speech and Harry looks at Meghan with tears in the corners of his eyes and speaks to Meghan in a feeble voice and almost chokes up.

It's not what real love's like, Em's mum says to Em. She sighs and switches it off, and Em's eyes are moist. Oh, dear! It's not real, you know! It's not really like that, her mum says, to comfort her.

She wants to try and talk about what happened before Em was born, she thinks it might be important. In what way? She's not sure, it's just that when the baby comes it could stir up some dregs. She's got a little wooden box painted black that she wants Emily to see. It goes back to Em's dad, it's basically the only thing she's kept, and maybe when it gets older the baby might want to keep little items of jewellery and baby teeth and locks of hair in it. I'd have died if I'd carried on living with him, Em's mum says. But I've not forgotten, I can't just forget him. She knows that Em's dad is a big black hole in Em's life, she knows that Em must have all sorts of questions she's been keeping in, questions that in a way have become solid inside her, but now with the baby on its way they're questions that might well be asked again. Em's mum has lots of things she wants to share. After all, I was on my own with you, she says, so I've done this before. It's all right to ask, she says softly, to herself or to Em, who isn't listening anyway (she says a lot of things that aren't much use). Em smoothes a hand over her tummy, more lying down on the sofa than sitting, her eyes more closed than open.

It takes a long time before Em has the courage to start asking those questions. Often they're hard, like little plastic pellets from a toy gun. Where was my dad when I was born? for instance. Or, Why didn't he want to be with us? And these are questions her mum can't answer.

That Em would make the same mistake was something she hadn't imagined, she's appalled by Em and disappointed with herself when she thinks about it, it's exactly like the parents of a boy in Em's class that were drug addicts and now the lad's a drug addict himself. Em's mum actually jumps when she sees her grey-white face in the mirror, and the longer she stands there, in front of the mirror, the faster her heart beats. How small a newborn baby is, hardly bigger than her hand, how's Em going to cope with being a mother, what if Em loses her temper and spits in the baby's face, what if Em grips the baby so tight that something breaks?

Every now and then her fears loom so large she feels she's at her wits' end and has to lie down on the floor. There are some things a mother can never admit or show to anyone, for example that ten years ago she ironed all Em's tops and trousers in case anyone got the idea of reporting her to the child welfare services.

At such weak moments, Em's mum feels like she's sinking through the carpet and the floorboards, down through all the floors. At such moments, Em's mum says to herself, You're good enough, you're good enough, you're good enough, you're good enough …

It's the first Thursday in March when he realises the staircase hasn't been washed down yet, there's still some dried-up kebab sauce on the top step of his landing. He goes down the stairs, down to the letter boxes, and with a blue biro puts a cross in the column next to her name on the cleaning roster. He takes her turn, but keeps it to himself, fetches the bucket from the cupboard and fills it up with water and detergent, starts on the sixth floor, outside her door, and works his way down to the ground floor. It's the least he can do. She always looks so down when he runs into her in the lift, a forlorn-looking face in grey and white, with hollow cheeks. Seen from the outside the neighbour's a good neighbour (inside not so much), he looks out for those around him, washes the stairs, picks up litter, says hello to all the children, fills the planters outside the entrance door with soil and plants flowers in them in the spring. Yes, he thinks to himself, Emily's life is a lot easier thanks to him.

He can spend hours making figures of eight with the mop, starting at the top on the sixth floor, working his way down, until eventually he steps into the lift and washes the floor there too, then cleans the mirror. After washing the whole staircase he finds he's been thinking about Emily so long he has to go to the bathroom. He imagines Emily putting out various items in the supermarket, heavy items on the lower shelves, she has to bend down, her back towards him, and she's not pregnant anymore. The way her body looks in detail is something he struggles to picture, is she thinner or fuller underneath her clothes, is her stomach firm, are her thighs flabbier than he's been thinking? Does he really have a thing about her? Her calves, her wrists, her broad shoulders? Can a person have a thing about someone they don't know? Perhaps not. He can sit on his sofa and think about her shoulders for minutes at a time before he's able to get up again. He knocks on her door, once, twice in fact, but there's no answer. He decides to write her another note, takes a sheet of thick white writing paper from the drawer, writes his note on it, drops it in her letter box, and takes the lift back up again. It's Friday night, he's been thinking about Emily and her big swollen tummy, so big she is now, and he's thought about how she holds her hands under her tummy when she goes down the stairs, both hands, he's seen her go down the stairs with both hands supporting her tummy, whereas she ought rather to keep hold of the handrail, because Emily could easily fall, she could tumble down the stairs and land on her tummy and damage the baby, and he'd have to do something then, What if I have to do something, he thinks, call the ambulance, stay with Emily in the ambulance, I'm her neighbour, he'd say, I heard a commotion on the stairs and went out to see, and there she was lying there, this pregnant girl, and at the hospital they'd ask him to wait outside the treatment room, or outside the operating theatre, because the baby would have to be delivered by cesarean, and during the time Emily was still asleep he'd be the one who'd have to hold the baby.

He's at his office, he works at the church in … Sinsen, Romsås, Ammerud … is there a church there? He's written something, a sermon, and he's about to hold one of the obligatory sessions for those getting confirmed, they're going to dramatise something from the Bible. He doesn't know what to say to them, they just sit there, or stand, in a semicircle, with tired looks of uncertainty (or certainty?), not wondering about anything, no one putting their hand up. He can't concentrate, he's got a headache, a headache thumping in his left temple, though only on the one side, does that make it psychological, he doesn't know. He watches some videos on his computer, about fitness (?), about cars (?), then after half an hour one about dating, a man talking about how men need smart, intelligent, stable women who respect certain qualities in a man, women who've known strong male role models. He doesn't really understand what it means, but the man explains that women without fathers, for example, can end up stripping for a living.

Emily's just a fantasy, it's all something he's made up, isn't it? Anyway, Emily would only think of him as a sort of father figure, even though father figure isn't a word she would use. He's back in his flat again, home from work. Or would she? Doesn't he think about his own age? Is it usual for someone to think the kinds of thoughts he thinks about her, about someone they don't actually know, he asks himself. He looks around his flat, at the furniture (worn?), the fridge (old?), he doesn't want to live here for ever, this isn't the place he'd imagined himself living, he wants to live in the city, a place with a balcony, but he's got a balcony, only he doesn't mean that sort of grey concrete balcony, but a nice one with black railings.

From his balcony, he can see the valley. The high-rise blocks out at Trosterud, Tveita, the railway lines, endless industrial sprawl.

Only once before in his life had he ever declared his love to anyone. In a way, this is the pastor's story, or his fate. It was to a female friend of his when he was nineteen, and the girl, who was from the south of the country, the Sørland, actually wanted to move in with him, but before that, she said, we have to get married. Her parents smiled and were amenable enough, but when he got to the matter in hand, whether they'd be inclined to give their daughter's hand in marriage, her father had replied that they were expecting someone from a rather different background, they'd forbidden their daughter to go out with a boy from Oslo's city centre when she was younger, but since they could no longer stand in her way now that she was an adult, they had to accept that she could go with whoever she wanted, there was nothing they could do about it, but that didn't mean they gave their blessing. The girl's mother had patted the neighbour on the shoulder and told him he'd be best off finding someone else, and had smiled cautiously then, her expression revealing what could almost have been pity (?).

But they never married, not because of her parents, it just never got to that point. And he's always thought his relationship with that well-off Jesus girl went so fast it ruined any other he might have had. For that reason he's been living on his own ever since. Slowly but surely, his bachelor life turned into his only life, which suited him fine.

It's strange what living alone does to a person; they fall into habits, like eating very quickly or touching their crotch all the time.

When her baby bump became noticeable, he wasn't disappointed, he felt glad. And why would that be, exactly? He's not certain, but as you'll doubtless know, sometimes you can be glad without being able to help it, and it's not unknown for a young person, for instance, to be glad when the person they're infatuated with finds someone else, it's almost a relief.

Now he's standing outside the supermarket where she works.

He kept looking at her while he was still inside, she came and joined the queue behind him at the checkout, she had her green work uniform on, but she also had a bag and a coat, which he took to mean she was on her way home. Yes. He hangs around outside and watches her as the cashier scans her items. He looks at her, he smiles at her, and she smiles back (but Emily doesn't know why she smiles, she just does, it's like her face won't, won't relax), and when she comes outside he's standing waiting for her. He says he just had to talk to her, and she carries on smiling, she asks if there's anything the matter, and he says no, it's just that they live in the same block, on the same staircase, and he thinks she looks nice, he's often wanted to talk to her, lots of times. She doesn't get what he's talking about, she thinks she meets the neighbour all the time, she thinks he's always going in and out of his flat.

And standing there in front of her, with only a metre or two between them, he doesn't look at her, it's because he can't, it's because the eye contact makes him nervous and he doesn't know where to look then. He looks at the trees, he pinches his nose and twists his body to face the supermarket.

She fiddles with her hair, plaits her hair as she

speaks. Most people would probably find it quite an annoying habit, but he doesn't.

He asks if perhaps, if perhaps she might be hungry, if perhaps she'd fancy a bite to eat, a place near the precinct perhaps, somewhere like that. And she, not knowing any better, says yes, and he says in that case he'd better just pop back home and get rid of his shopping. She stands outside and waits for him. When he comes back out he's got a different pair of shoes on, pointed, shiny leather (he's made an effort).

The way he walks there beside Emily anyone would think it was his baby she was carrying.

It's not a café, only a kind of cafeteria, a lot of people from the nearby offices go there for their lunch and sit at the long tables. But now they're the only ones there, them and two or three building workers.

And what do they talk about? They haven't actually got much to say. But they talk about work and about food, she has a yoghurt, he has a prawn sandwich, You probably aren't allowed to eat this, he says, and she doesn't know one way or the other, she says, I don't like prawns. When Em talks and eats at the same time, she hides her mouth with her arm, she pulls her sweater sleeves down over her hands too, as if she's got scars.

When's her baby due? Less than two months now. Does she mind if he asks where her boyfriend is? No, we're not together anymore, she says. She feels so sorry for him, the shoes he's wearing (!), that she can't bring herself to pretend she's got a boyfriend, and when, after they've eaten, he places a hand between her shoulder blades, she lets him keep it there.

Is there anything about Emily's circumstances that could make the birth more difficult?

Is Emily dependent on any medication?

Is Emily suffering from any illness, has she been depressed, has she experienced recurrent depressive episodes, has she been subjected to abuse or assault?

It's the stupid midwife asking these questions (WHY?), they're just standard questions that have to be asked, that need to be ticked off in the questionnaire, things that are good to know. The midwife enters her measurements of Emily's tummy into her computer, then notes them down on Emily's health card. Yellow light, posters on the walls, the midwife with powder-red lipstick on today, a soft face, soft hands on Emily's tum, and now hands that are placed on her knees. Oh, these trustworthy health workers who make her want to tell everything! She struggles a bit with her words, thought she had a feeling of, no, that's not right, she doesn't know what she thought or felt, numbness, maybe? Is that something you can feel, she asks, and the midwife nods, because the midwife knows what buttons to press to make things come pouring out of the mouths of pregnant women. These are just things that are important for us to know prior to a birth, because they can affect the way you cope with having your baby. Do you understand? says the midwife.

Em looks up at the ceiling.

Em does remember Pablo hitting her once, but only a slap on the cheek, and only the once. That won't be what they mean, so it's not what she says, no one cares about a slap in the face, what they want is something Em's kept hidden, for years, something she's now meant to retrieve and talk about, after which she can hide it away again, for years.

Em also remembers one of her uncles putting one, two, maybe three fingers inside her while she was sunbathing at a family get-together when she was fifteen. A family get-together? Yes, it was someone's birthday, out on some farm or other. At first, her uncle had massaged her legs, starting at her ankles, then gradually his hands moved further and further up, until at last he pulled her bikini bottoms down. He'd felt her bum and then his fingers moved towards her crotch. She kicked out at him after he'd done it. Her bikini bottoms were pink with frills along the edge, and for some reason Em's kept them, they're in a cardboard box in the bedroom somewhere, or no, she'll have got rid of them, why would she keep something like that?

It doesn't hurt to talk, but she starts feeling dizzy and the midwife fetches her a glass of water, the midwife writes even more things down in her notepad this time, but her handwriting's so small Emily can't see what she puts. When her appointment's over, she walks all the way home, the day feels strange to her, it's like one of those days that just go daft on you, she's shaking and exhausted, sleeps long into the afternoon and has trouble falling asleep again at bedtime. But does any of it have any bearing? No, before long she feels normal again, before long all this is no more than a tick on a questionnaire she takes with her to the maternity ward, it's forgotten by the midwife and forgotten again by Emily.

It's the next day and Emily looks at herself in the mirror. She's so quiet, with her tears and her dreams, why can't she say anything?

And hasn't she got a hobby? She's very good with makeup and hair, she uses five different skin products every day, and if she wanted she could most probably have done a cosmetics course and become a beautician specialising in skincare or brows.

The sun comes out, though only for a bit, as Em stands waiting for the metro to come, it shines right in her face, she gleams and narrows her eyes to see in the direction it'll be coming from. Em's mum is in the kitchen, washing up after a lunch consisting of porridge as she stares out of the window, looking down at the metro station, but she doesn't see Em down there. The porridge turned out thick, it blocks the plughole in the sink. When she's finished the dishes she goes down to fetch the post and leaves the bills unopened in a little pile in the kitchen. She doesn't know what to do with the other letters at first, they're for Pablo. Five in all. She decides to put them in a plastic bag she then puts away in one of the cupboards.

It's almost four by the time Em gets into work, there's three of them on today, Em and Marewan and Tina, who today touches Em's cheek and gives her a big hug, Em can smell her perfume. It's our last day on the job together! Tina says. She asks if she can have a feel, and places a very cautious hand on Em's tummy, so cautious that Em has to press down on it so it's a proper feel. After that she takes her place on the checkout. She can't remember all the codes anymore for the fruit and veg, and blames it on being pregnant (I forget such a lot of things because of this belly), whenever someone wants a vegetable she has to shout for Tina. Tina has to come with the log-in card too on several occasions, because Em makes too many scanning errors to be able to rectify things herself using Void Item, which sets one of the customers off in a rage: It's not the first time you've entered things twice, what kind of a scam is this? Em taps her finger up and down on the receipt key and hands the customer five receipts. What's this supposed to mean, the customer says, trying to embarrass me now, are you? And at that point the word cow slips from Em's mouth and the customer storms off with her paprika and cheese in a see-through carrier bag, ranting on about reporting her to the manager. Afterwards Marewan calls Em into the office, asks her to sit down, It's your last day, he says, you should take things easy, he says. Marewan. He puts the kettle on, takes a mug out of the cupboard, drops a tea bag in it, and pours the boiling water over. Forget about her, Marewan says at first. A lot of customers aren't right in the head, you know there's a social security office just round the corner, don't you? Anyway, it wasn't a regular customer who does all their shopping here, those are the ones we don't want to lose.

Marewan stirs a lump of coconut fat into Em's tea, to lubricate the colon, you'll be blocking up by now, I imagine, he says with a wink. Little globs float in slowly slackening circles inside the mug.

It's three minutes before closing when a customer comes in for a big shop, Em has to scan in more than twenty items, over five hundred kroner in total, and by then it's four minutes past eleven, and the customer just stands there grinning. Em says nothing, but she's really tired, and the customer, a man in his forties, feels he's got to say something out loud, he says, You're not closed yet, not until I'm done. The man looks down his nose at Em as he enters his PIN, while Marewan stands ready, follows the customer out, and locks the door behind him. Marewan then takes the money, while Em balances the till, there's a shortage today too, a hundred and three kroner, flashing lamps and beeping sounds from the register.

It's knocking on for midnight by the time Em and Marewan switch the lights off and let themselves out of the shop. Marewan still in his green uniform, they get into Marewan's car and he drives her up to Carl Berner, or to Tøyen, somewhere she can catch the metro. Em closes her eyes, her head feels heavy and for a moment she falls asleep, everything goes completely dark, and then there are lights, it's cold, and she's getting out of the car.

Look at Emily, she's all curled up. She's been asleep, she hasn't moved since the day before, when she climbed into bed exhausted and closed her eyes exactly like a poor person.

Em's mum decides she'll go with Em down to the metro station when it's time for Em to go to her send-off before stopping work (she must have changed her mind), the path's so slippery Em could easily fall flat on her tummy, and she knows of a woman who fell down a hole in the pavement and lost her baby, the family wept their hearts out, gathered around the little bundle in the incubator with all its wires attached. Em holds tight onto her mum's coat as they go down the hill, abrupt little tugs at her coat, her mum concentrates on keeping steady. They stand and wait for the train to come. Em wanders up and down the platform instead of taking the weight off her feet on one of the benches. Her mum wonders why Emily can't sit down and be still, it wears her out, watching her daughter go backwards and forwards like that. When Em gets on the train and sits down in one of the bays of four face-to-face seats, Em's mum waves from the platform. She thinks about the money she's saved up for a holiday abroad one day, which she'll now have to give to Emily and the baby, the maternity pay won't amount to much. She's hardly ever been to Spain, just the once with her mates when Emily was two, but she'd have loved to have gone back to lie on a beach with sunglasses on and sip a drink or visit a vineyard. She used to be slim once, and strong, her arms were evenly tanned. And on the spur of the moment one time she bought tickets for the Denmark boat, went and picked Emily up from her playgroup, went barging in, if truth be told, and shouted across the room: Look, Emily! We're going to Denmark! On the boat, they sat and listened to a live band and Emily had a blue drink bought for her by a fat man who came up and asked if he could dance with her mum. The man whispered in Em's mum's ear while they danced, and Emily had sat there empty-eyed with her blue umbrella drink.

She thinks it best to stay awake and wait up for Emily, so she watches TV and makes herself something to eat, she cleans the kitchen and hasn't a clue how they're going to cope with having a baby, she's exhausted enough as it is and the baby hasn't even been born yet. When Emily lets herself in just after ten, she's already fallen asleep on the sofa.

Marewan buys a six-pack of beer per person, he puts them all in the fridge and upends a bag of crisps into a bowl. He's drunk half a can before Jørgen arrives and he gets up to welcome him with a hand out in greeting. Then come the rest of the staff, Ramesh (Marewan's brother), Håkon, Nadia, Tina, but only Tina and Håkon want a beer, Ramesh is driving and asks how many Marewan's planning on having, I'll be driving you home too by the looks of it, he says with a grin. Emily arrives ten minutes before the minibus is due to pick them up, and drinks a glass of coke. She's wearing black tights and a skirt, or is it a dress, probably tight underneath her woolly sweater, certainly tight from her hips down to her knees. Marewan stares until he realises he's staring, then turns to the crisps.

When Emily goes on the sick from tomorrow and after that on maternity leave, Ramesh's wife will take over her job. It'll make it look like a family business, something Marewan hadn't envisaged, and he's not sure if it's a good thing having so many of his own family working in the shop.

Jørgen's put makeup on, some black around his eyes, shiny lips that make slippery smacking sounds. Emily leans across to Jørgen and dabs the corner of his mouth with a finger to wipe something away, his lip gloss has run, she says, and then says something else too that Marewan doesn't catch. Jørgen says he's going to miss her, Marewan says Emily'll be back, Emily says she's going to miss them, Marewan says that if she can sort out a babysitter then maybe she'd like to take part in the Super-KIWI convention in May, they get everything paid for, and she says yes, yes, if I can. She lets them put their hands on her tummy one by one. Jørgen's already drunk and wants them to feel his as well, so Nadia puts her ear to his stomach and says she can hear something. Jørgen says Em's so young, and lucky for it, her body, her tits, will soon look the same as before.

At the bowling centre her belly gets in the way, she can hardly keep her balance and can only drop the bowling ball into the lane instead of rolling it. She watches it bounce heavily a couple of times before it skitters off into the gutter and somehow gets stuck at the far end. It happens more than once, and they have to press the button each time so a staff member can come and retrieve the ball for her. Em says sorry, but the staff member just gives her a look of exasperation. Eventually she asks Jørgen to take her goes for her and sits down on the sofa for a rest. Short, delicate breaths that are barely breaths at all.

In the evenings Em can hear the people in the flat next door through the wall. They talk in loud voices, argue, have sex, have other people round, play loud music. She thinks about Pablo, his mole and his yellow hue. The radiator drips for hours, the air in the bedroom gets dense and humid. Em imagines stroking Pablo's back. He always lies with his back to her. She imagines him breathing heavily, Em stroking with the tips of her fingers and a bit with just the nails, maybe he'll stir, but as she imagines it he's sound asleep. She fetches an apple from the kitchen, cuts it into wedges, takes the wedges back with her to the bedroom, crunching loudly with her mouth open, and her mum gives a jump on the sofa. The baby turns inside her belly, it feels like it's squirming, not the same movements as when it punches or kicks, they're bigger and bulkier than that. It actually hurts a bit.

Her phone rings tonight and when she picks it up it's Pablo, she thinks now they ought to talk about the feelings they have for each other, the feelings she has for him, this hopeless relationship (this wasp sting, red and tender). Pablo says hi, his voice always sounds so flat and uninterested. He says he's only got three minutes, Em hasn't time to ask why, he tells her he's got to keep a low profile for a while yet. She knows she ought to ask him about the appointment with the doctor, why he didn't come, and tell him he's got to sign the acknowledgement of paternity before the baby's born, so that he can't just run away from it all, but she can't get any of this out, all she says is, Why haven't you phoned before now, it's all she gets to say before he's telling her he got stopped by the police for wearing new trainers.

Em and the midwife (the one she told about being sexually abused that time) sat for a few minutes waiting for Pablo to come, the midwife drummed her fingers on the desk before eventually she said, No, we'll have to come back to this later. He can still sign when the baby comes, she explained, and stood up to signal that the appointment was over and it was time for Em to leave. And then, as she showed Em towards the door: If the father won't acknowledge paternity, there's always the courts. That'll require blood tests from you all, the baby gets a little jab in the foot, and the father will be required to attend by law. If he doesn't, the police (uniformed) will come and get him and take him to the hospital for a DNA test. I'm sure you'll get things sorted out before it comes to that, she said in the doorway, look after yourself in the meantime.

EM CHOOSES A NAME

One day when Marewan was talking to her, his morning breath was warm and dense, she threw up.

That's how it starts.

Then you're waking up at nights to stuff yourself with biscuits.

Afterwards she goes to the chemist's to buy a pregnancy test, and there, among the shelves, with her head down, because maybe she's ashamed of herself or thinks it's embarrassing (there's always an element of shame in buying a pregnancy test), she eventually finds the tests in the section for intimate hygiene, alongside hair removal creams, condoms, menstrual pads, and suppositories. The chemist asks in a loud voice if there's anything she can help her with, and Em says, I'm looking for a test, and the chemist, now a saleswoman, shows Em an expensive one and a cheap one. Are you familiar with testing, the woman asks with acne all over her face, her voice a monotone. Yes, Em lies. So you don't need me to tell you what to do, the woman says. No, Em lies. She puts the test in her bag and decides not to think any more about it until the next morning, and doesn't either, instead she drinks her last beer, or cider, because she doesn't like beer. The red cider bubbles in her glass and Em thinks the baby must be a dark little squiggle that looks like a tadpole.

Shortly after that she pees on the tip of the testing stick, re-caps it, and looks away for as long as she can. Longer than five minutes. She paces the floor in the kitchen and when after eight minutes she removes the cap and sees the two coloured bands she isn't filled with joy, nor with despair, but with a feeling that's hard to put into words. Is it anxiety she feels? Is it indifference? Emptiness? Is that a feeling?

All her life Emily's had dreams, big empty ones, blurred and unfocused, one thought shoving the other aside, after a lesson at school the only thing in her exercise book would be a big block letter with thick edges and a pattern of dots inside that she'd coloured in. And her teacher could then say to her mother at her parents' night, after politely having asked Emily to go outside into the corridor, that Emily wasn't paying attention, that Emily possibly had learning difficulties, even though that wasn't the case.

Em dreams about the baby, she can already see herself, looking at her swollen tummy in the mirror with no clothes on, and she sees herself with a baby in her arms as well. But Pablo doesn't want a baby (DREADING it already), they've got nothing in place, are they actually going to have a baby, is it going to live in this little flat? You can get pregnant when you want in a few years' time, he says, I just don't want a baby now, I'll give you ten grand not to have it, and so on and so on, he says. After reading up on the internet Em decides this is what all young men say, because the baby is something bewildering and incomprehensible to them.

Still, in week eight she goes to the outpatient clinic in the hospital basement to get an abortion. And while she's sitting there with the yellow abortion document in her hand a woman comes up to her who hasn't got a yellow document but who's there anyway for whatever reason, and says to Emily in English, God bless you, sweet child. Unsettled, Em sits on her chair until her name is called out. In the nurse's office she's handed a glass of water, a pill for now, and some more for later. And luckily she hesitates long enough not to put that pill in her mouth.

Because Pablo can say what he wants.

And the midwife says the baby that's in her tummy has chosen Em over everyone else to be its mother.

She can see the baby already, in Em's tummy.

Em chooses a name. She chooses a cot and a cupboard and a changing table on the internet, a van comes and delivers them, the driver puts everything in the lift and carries it all inside for her into her flat. She chooses the baby's appearance too: her own skin colour, Pablo's hair, and dark eyes.

It's more than six months ago now that Em felt a prickly sensation inside her, and although the baby was only a blob of slime then, it prickled nevertheless, like a tadpole (a tadpole wouldn't prickle, so maybe wriggled or shimmied).

Then at last her tummy begins to swell, there's something moving in there, Em strokes her tummy and must actively encourage Pablo to put his hand there. Come here and have a feel. Can you feel it, the baby's turning round now. The baby's got the hiccups. Can you feel it?

Being at work makes the time go so quickly, Em thinks, back and forth she goes and the day's suddenly gone.

Em's mum's in the supermarket getting something for her dinner when Em phones and says her contractions have started and it'd be good if her mum would come to the hospital and sit with her, Em's voice is a bit feeble. Or no, that's not how it happens, she speaks hurriedly, Mum, you've got to come now, she says, and hangs up straight away, her mum hardly manages to get a word in, she just stands there in the middle of the supermarket with her mouth open, at a loss. She wants me to come, she wants me there, Em's mum has to tell herself, like the poorest kid in school who at long last can afford to go to a classmate's birthday party and take some money with her for a present. In the midst of that quivering moment she loses touch with herself and drops a tub of soured cream on the floor, causing it to split open, stands there, bewildered and stupid, and wonders what to do, whether she'll have to pay for it and clean it off the floor herself, or whether a young staff member will come and say not to worry, they'll sort it out, no, she leaves her items, the salmon and some other things on a pallet of chocolates that are on offer, and goes outside where it occurs to her that she ought to have bought some nappies. So she goes back in and buys all the packets they've got in size 1, then goes out again and wonders whether to get a taxi, decides to get a taxi and waves her hand at each one that passes, not knowing whether the lit-up sign means occupied or free. In the taxi she asks the driver to take her to the hospital, she says she's going to be a grandmother, and the taxi driver says, oh, really, and is totally disinterested, but she doesn't notice.

Em turns up at the hospital, at the A&E, four days before the baby's due, she's already been on the phone to the hospital, she's brought her bag of things and ordered a taxi, done her breathing the whole way there, breathing in, then slowly out, and the taxi driver said he didn't think it had started yet, she was that calm and quiet, only she didn't catch what he said, all she could do was breathe. The woman at the reception desk at the hospital peers at her from behind her glasses and can't see Em's tummy because Em's got her big hoodie on and is leaning towards the desk to tell the woman she's arrived, I'm here now, she says, and the woman asks what she's here for, if she's got an appointment or if she's phoned beforehand, and Em shouts, everyone can hear her, that she's gone into labour! After that she's taken, led by the hand by the receptionist woman, all the way to the maternity ward where a midwife and a nurse come to take care of her, Em can't remember what the midwife's called, or the nurse, but they're with her the whole time after that.

Whenever a contraction comes, Em breathes slowly out and counts the seconds in her mind. Sometimes she counts up to sixty before her tummy relaxes.

And whenever a contraction comes, she thinks again about Pablo going off in the evenings with his holdall, she sees herself waiting for him on the sofa, hours and days, or else she's standing in the bathroom looking at herself in the mirror, picking at her own skin, standing there so long that at some point she probably forgot all about Pablo, like when someone dies and you wake up the next day and have forgotten they're no longer alive. How can someone just go off like that? Is he meant to just come in through the door again, is that what she thought? And what then, what's meant to happen then?

The midwife's Danish, with gleaming white teeth, Em really wants to tell her what nice teeth she's got, she wants to feel what they're like with her tongue. The midwife says Em's going to have an uncomplicated birth, a bit like a cat having kittens, but Em can't quite catch what she says, it's her mum who has to tell her a bit later on that she's to go down on all fours and push. The midwife goes over to a monitor, reads what it says, and writes something down on a sheet of paper, then she comes back with her midwife's stethoscope and presses it against Em's tum. The midwife looks at the monitor, talks to Em, and not long afterwards she's listening with her stethoscope nearly every minute, but now Em's got to rest a bit between the contractions, the midwife tells her firmly, and Em's mum moves closer, she's been sitting on a chair in the corner.

Em's mum would so much like to say something soothing, she's asked to give Em some squash to drink from the jug, she steps right up to the bed then and holds the glass in front of Em, who drinks from it with a straw. After that, Em's mum puts a hand to Em's brow, she's standing so very close now, talking to her through her breath, There's a good girl, she says, and Em vomits.

She imagines Pablo being with another woman, Pablo thinking about a woman in a black dress, not Em but that fat Irina who played in goal at football practice and never let a single goal in. She's so exhausted she's got no control over her body anymore, look how her legs and arms tremble, she can't stand on her own two feet and can't lie on her back either, she can't bear to have clothes on, can't drink the squash, the nurse has to remove all Em's clothes for her while Em cries, and then Em has to go down on all fours. The baby's coming out now.

Fatherless babies aren't exactly welcome in the same way as normal babies, no one ever really asked for them, it's not as if they're celebrated with pink balloons the way other babies are. But still the midwife cries out when the baby comes: LOOK AT THIS BEAUTIFUL BABY!

The baby's hardly been born before it's on top of her, devouring her. The baby cries a lot.

Em's mum says the baby's feeding just right, and the midwife, before closing the door of the big empty room where they'll spend the night, says the baby's feeding so well she thinks they'll not get a wink of sleep, the baby'll keep them awake, perhaps it'll sleep at the breast, but not on its own, in its own cot.

The baby is given a name, Em says it out loud, and the midwife writes the name down with a lot of hearts on a blue strip she attaches to the plastic cot.

Em chose the name ages ago, she chose it all the way back when she was at school, she feels like it's her own.

The first night, the baby cries a lot, Em lifts him up (but be careful with his head, you must always be careful with his head), puts him to the breast, takes him from the breast, puts him to the breast again, and after a while, when the baby's fallen asleep, at the breast, she tries to move him over to his cot, only then he cries again. Em's mum stirs in her armchair in the corner, she gets to her feet and comes over, picks up the baby and holds him close to her own chest, only the baby keeps on crying, and Em snaps at her mum because he won't stop. I can't sleep with all his noise, Em weeps. Her body is so exhausted her legs won't stop shaking. She tells her mum to take the baby somewhere else and leave her in peace.

Em's mum doesn't quite know what to do to calm the baby down, she can't remember what she did with Em, she thinks she might remember what it felt like to hold Em, but she'd forgotten all about this terrible crying.

She's surprised by the baby's big abdomen and thin legs. Perhaps he's got a sore tummy? She thinks he looks a bit like an insect and presses gently on his tummy while changing his nappy, to see if it's flatulence or whether he's just full.

The corridor is quiet, but she can hear other babies crying behind other doors, and now and again she sees a nurse go in or out, or mothers leaving their rooms to get some crispbread or squash. Further along, a baby lies crying in an illuminated cot.

Em's baby is so little, her mum has to be careful, she must keep tight hold even though the baby wriggles and squirms. He cries all the time while he's awake, and she must rock him as she walks the corridor.

Back in the "maternity hotel," as the section's rightly called, Em asks her mum why she's not saying anything, and Em's mum hushes her, she's got to be quiet, What for, says Em, stroppy, as if it's an inconvenience to her that her mum's being so quiet, she doesn't get this, why do they have to be quiet, they've got their own room, haven't they? So as not to frighten the baby, her mum whispers, You being angry like that might distress him. Em says the baby needs to learn about noise and get used to it. Em's mum sighs and says there's a difference between angry sounds and normal sounds, she read somewhere that babies can tell. She heard about a child once that couldn't tell the difference anymore between laughter and fighting, the child thought it was a game and clapped its hands together with glee whenever the parents fought.

Now you've had a shower, you've felt the hot water sprinkle down on your head, now you know, Emily, what childbirth's like, and your skin's still tingling.

Her belly's gone after only a few hours, Em looks normal again, she must touch her flat stomach the whole time just to make sure.

Can she smell her baby too, can she smell it's hers?

She feels a tightness in her abdomen, it hurts.

She doesn't really know yet how she'll talk and sing to the baby. She thinks the baby won't remember anything she says anyway.

At one point while she's still in the hospital Em goes to the canteen to get some dinner, she's so hungry, she trundles the baby in front of her in his plastic cot and prays to God he'll stay asleep. In the canteen an older mother, fortyish, breastfeeds her baby while eating. The woman smiles at her, only Emily doesn't notice, she's busy eating up her meatloaf as fast as she can, and holds her breath every time her baby moves.

Before they go home Em has to breastfeed the baby to sleep, and between the first boob and the second a nurse gives the child milk from a cup and calls it "topping up." The nurse fetches Em's records too and asks her to contact the health centre and make an appointment with the midwife there. And, oh yes, she reminds her, though in a friendly way, the father still has to acknowledge paternity. But you'll be aware of that from earlier, the nurse says before the taxi arrives.

Em's mum is so filled with love she keeps going over to the cot to look at the baby, just to look at him.

He sleeps with his lips slightly parted, his arms above his head, and now he's sleeping soundly.

Every morning, Em's mum comes into the bedroom, Em'll be lying on her side with her arm around her baby, his mouth clamped around her breast, but now he's just let go. They're asleep, the two of them together, and Em's mum lifts the baby up, holds the baby to her own chest, and goes into the living room with him, goes from one end of the room to the other with him for a good many minutes, with one arm under the baby's bottom, her other hand flat against his back, until the baby settles against her chest, nuzzles, rests his head heavily against her chest, Emily's mum's. She says out loud, But I've got no milk. She goes backwards and forwards with the baby before sitting down and rocking him gently from side to side while she sits.

Perhaps because she feels sorry for her, perhaps to comfort her, Em's mum tells Em the baby doesn't need feeding more than every four hours, she says this a couple of days after they've been allowed to go home from the hospital, Em's hardly slept, her mum can tell she needs to rest, her hands are shaking and her eyes are glazed. She looks like she's going to cry! All Em's mum wants is to help, but who is she exactly to be saying things like that, every four hours, it's tantamount to child abuse, at least that's what the midwife at the health centre (sexual abuse story) would surely have said, because it's up to the baby itself when it wants feeding and Em should actually be offering her breast whenever the baby opens its mouth or starts sucking on his own hand! But the baby does these things all the time, nearly every ten minutes the baby's been putting his hand in his mouth, over and over again, which means Em has to feed him all the time and it hurts like mad when he sucks the way he does.

They draw all the curtains, switch off the lights, the dark'll be best for the baby.

A midwife comes to check on them and tells them sternly to let some light in, he needs daylight!

She claps her hands, claps for Em and her milk, she says Em could be producing for a whole maternity unit and it's quite normal, all she has to do is put the baby to her breast more often. The baby opens his mouth only a few seconds, not wide enough to make room for a nipple, and Em's sore, she's not in any hurry either. The midwife's standing next to her, watching as Em puts the baby to her breast, That's right, she says. But it hurts, says Em (she's so nervous). You're doing fine, says the midwife. Afterwards, she weighs the baby, she puts a weighing scale down on the floor with a paper towel unfolded on the flat surface where the baby's to be put. Em's mum takes off all the baby's clothes (nervously, movements a bit severe), his nappy too, and places him on the scale, it looks like such a harsh thing to do, Em thinks, he's crying, and the midwife says, Oh, what a cross little boy, and presses a key. She presses the key again and writes the figure down. She looks at the chart from the hospital, then gets her phone out and taps a few times. She says the baby's not putting on weight as much as would be ideal, that he's eleven per cent down on his weight at birth. But she says too that it's quite normal for them to lose a little weight to begin with. She says all this in a calm and gentle voice. Em's mum tells her the baby feeds often, he can be at it for hours, and the midwife says it's not unusual for a baby not to be feeding optimally. Em can't understand it, she doesn't know where she's gone wrong. The midwife has a look round the flat, she inspects the pram, the bed, the changing table, the kettle they use to sterilise the teats, she goes into the bathroom and shuts the door, and Em can hear her (she thinks) opening the cupboards, and the pedal bin to count the used nappies, and then the midwife comes out again, she asks about the nappies and doesn't seem quite as unconcerned now. Before she leaves, she wants to see Em put the baby to her breast one more time. Em sits down on the sofa, her mum hands her a cushion and then puts the baby down on it, and Em squeezes a bit of milk out onto the baby's nose, which makes the baby open his mouth, and after two or three goes she manages to get her nipple between his lips.

Everything seems to be fine, the midwife says, she'll come back the next day and they'll weigh the baby again, she says in her gentle, soothing voice, it's nothing to be worried about, but maybe they should move the bed a bit so the baby won't have to sleep in a draught from the window.

The next day, another midwife comes, not the same one as the day before, a new one this time, with dark hair, she talks very fast, but her Norwegian's not very good, Em's mum can't understand half of what she says, she's no idea where she might be from, whether it's a Spanish accent she's got or something else, Em's mum just stands there, she thinks she'll be at her wits' end before long, she feels so worn out, like an old woman. Emily carries the baby with a hand under his bottom, she goes round in circles while the midwife's talking, and nods at everything she says, her mum can't tell if Emily's actually taking any of it in, but Emily says the baby'll start sucking his hands again ten minutes after he's been fed and that she's up half the night with him. The midwife puts the weighing scale down on the floor at first, but doesn't seem happy with it and puts it on the kitchen worktop instead. Emily hands her the baby, without his nappy on, he cries the whole time, the midwife puts him on the scale, she notes down his weight and asks how much he weighed the day before, which Emily tells her, and the midwife then presses the key again. Oh, but that's not right, she exclaims, his weight's now 3.666 kilos, the other midwife must have weighed him wrong! (Weighed him wrong? How do you weigh a baby wrong?) They could have had the child welfare services let loose on them, Em's mum thinks. I thought it couldn't be right, Emily says, and puts the baby to her breast so the midwife can see she's doing nothing wrong, and the midwife watches and says Emily should grip her breast like a hamburger to shape it right, she demonstrates how by forming a C with her thumb and forefinger. Emily nods, but her mum doesn't understand what the midwife means, again she feels like a tree or something, standing in the background with its leaves all fluttering. The midwife weighs the baby again and writes the figure down, she says he just drank exactly sixty grams of milk, it means the baby's feeding, and Em's mum asks if those measurements are accurate, Are you sure it's right now, she says, and the midwife says Yes, yes, everything's right now. So everything's fine.

It feels like a day lasts as long as two. (Is this normal, is there anyone else besides Em who's felt the same way and can provide an explanation?) She tries to sleep when the baby sleeps, she wakes up with her mouth all dry and feeds the baby, her mouth feels even drier then, it literally feels like the baby's sucking all the fluid out of her body.

And she thinks to herself then that it's as if her womb is shrivelling up, she thinks too that the baby ought to have a father soon, as she carries him backwards and forwards, from one side of the room to the other, until he sleeps, and she sits down, and then he wakes, moves his head from side to side, left to right, right to left, and she has to get up again.

PABLO

Somewhere else is Pablo, somewhere down the road, among the orange-fronted housing blocks, but where exactly is a secret, he can't tell her. I can't tell you, he says, his voice is almost a shout, and Em sighs on the other end of the phone. Don't do that, says Pablo, just don't, you've got no reason, he says, and Em taps to end the call (but this is before the baby comes, the baby's still safe inside her tummy then). Now anyone would think Pablo might feel guilty because Em hung up on him, but no, not in the slightest, Pablo kicks a stone and sends it skidding along the pavement. By the time he's stopped being annoyed, Em's just a little squiggle somewhere at the back of his mind.

One day Ousman goes to see Pablo, Ousman says he's laid his hands on some dead-cheap piff (nicked from someone's stash, only Pablo doesn't know this).

But it's pure stuff, they sample the weed themselves, though Ousman already knows, he's used some already, and anyway it wouldn't be good business selling weed cut with something that might be dangerous. Pablo says he wants twenty per cent of the take on every bag he sells, but Ousman reckons Pablo's only entitled to fifteen, the other five per cent are costs, something Ousman calls his consultancy fee, which annoys Pablo already.

This is when Pablo goes out the door with a holdall slung over his shoulder for his stash, he shuts the door after him and Emily becomes even vaguer to him then, a figure, reclining or standing, floating or fluttering at the very back of his mind, waiting for him. It's not like she's going anywhere, Pablo tells himself, and thinks of her as a bulging black bin bag, or a sack that's just lying there.

Pablo sells nearly everything Ousman can supply him with, but he sticks to a circle of people he recognises, he sells to acquaintances who sell to acquaintances to acquaintances to acquaintances. Pablo soon has a lot of bank notes in his possession, he folds them up and hides them away among his things, and he gives Ousman a freebie that Ousman shares with some friends of his, but unfortunately they're the ones who got the weed nicked from their stash in the first place.

Pablo gets a phone call from Ousman. Ousman asks casually if Pablo's up for a late-night spliff.

Defo, says Pablo, but then, on his way to the spot where they're going to smoke, he sees a car and starts noiding (but thinks at first it's the weed that's noiding him).

It's a black car with the window rolled down, two lads (bad lads) from the area and Ousman in the back. Get in, they tell him.

Pablo gets in and hopes they're not going to break his nose before he's given them a name they can vent their anger on. They drive to somewhere quieter about twenty minutes away, where they point a taser in his face, that sort of thing, point it at his eye, his mouth, stick it in his ear ...

And soon after that they're on their way ...

To the place where the lads who stole the weed live.

Pablo knocks on the door, one of them looks through the spy hole and sees it's only Pablo. He opens the door for him, and the bad lads, who've been standing where they couldn't be seen, go barging in.

Baseball bats to the face, hands, body. They get the shit beaten out of them, the lad who came to the door and another one who'd tried to hide under the kitchen table, and not only that, they're handed penalties too, 100K each. Two thieving young stash-robbers with body and soul mashed to a pulp. They're given a month to repay. With text loans or whatever, a lot of stress and bootlicking, they'll get it sorted.

Pablo stands sheepishly looking on, and his eyes say sorry to the thieves while the bad lads lace into them ...

Once the assailants have gone, Pablo lifts one of the stash-robber lads up and puts him to bed so he can get some rest or get some sleep, neither of the two can walk on their own, and he helps the other onto the sofa. After all, he's nearly killed them in a way. He gets them each a coke out of the fridge, one of them drinks some, the other just lies there covered in blood. In the days that follow, Pablo makes them porridge, one of them can eat by himself, the other has to be fed.

On the street outside the flat stands Lily (proper slag's name), one of Pablo's many female acquaintances, though one he hasn't seen in nearly a year (?), or maybe two (?), not after she went off her head and hurled some drinking glasses at his TV, after that she was out on her arse.

She's dyed her hair lighter than it was before, now it's yellow, and she's wearing a black sleeveless top with no bra on underneath, Pablo can see the outline of her nipples, one of them's pierced, Horny bitch, Pablo thinks. But Lily isn't waiting for Pablo, it's Danny she's waiting for, and she's surprised when Pablo comes to the door, that's why she waves like that and crosses over and throws her arms around his neck. Lily asks if Pablo can lend her some money and Pablo's fingers curl around the notes in his trouser pocket. Come back tomorrow, I'll give you something then, he says, and Lily says, All right, I will, or something like that, and she says it again, just to make sure. Scenes play in Pablo's mind as he walks along the road, Lily with her pierced nipple, Lily with a can of coke stuck up her cunt, that sort of thing.

The police pick Pablo up after he's been to the supermarket for some milk, they're waiting for him outside BUNNPRIS when he comes out, a patrol car and everything.

They pat him down, check his pockets.

Pablo's sitting on a chair when the policewoman comes in, he's sitting uneasily. Now and then he extends his legs under the table. Now and then he leans over the desk and buries his face in his hands.

The policewoman asks a lot of questions and Pablo answers. He answers the same way whatever the question, firmly and to the point. She asks if he's been aware of anything out of the ordinary going on, anything he might have noticed while he's been buying and selling, if he knows Ousman, he's been in and out of that flat, they know that, but no, he doesn't. As soon as he is asked a question, Pablo shakes his head, before he even thinks about it. She wants to know what he's been doing with himself the last couple of years, but Pablo would prefer not to talk about the past.

Her main impression is that Pablo's scruffy and unwashed, there's something waxy and pale about his face, his trackie top looks too small for him and his fingernails are bitten to the quick, the cuticles are all frayed. She thinks men who've lived an easy life have something smooth about their faces, the skin wrinkles only behind the ears and a bit at the throat, but men who've lived a hard life have more furrows and drooping eyelids, which in a way makes Pablo stand out because he's so young, hardly more than a boy, and yet he's got those lines around his mouth.

She asks Pablo if he can tell her anything more about Ousman, when did he see Ousman last, didn't they used to be good friends, and Pablo says he'll tell her only if they can take a coffee break, but after the break he's not sure anymore and refuses to say anything. He sits there chewing the lip of his paper cup until it goes mushy, and he spits out little bits of pulp. Pablo wants a cigarette break now, but the policewoman tells him he can't. If we keep taking breaks all the time, we're never going to get anywhere. Have you changed your mind, is there anything more you know, she asks. Pablo says he's got no more to say, whether he talks or not it's going to land someone in it. Like who, the policewoman asks.

I don't need to answer that, do I. It's not like I've got to answer anything, says Pablo. No, that's right, says the policewoman. You're allowed not to say anything. But bear in mind that not saying anything can be taken in different ways.

It's morning, he feels like going and knocking on Ousman's door, because it's Ousman's fault the stash-robbers nearly got beaten to death, he wants to make Ousman feel it, feel what, Feel what needs to be felt, Pablo says. It's Danny asking, he's lying on the sofa with a tooth knocked out. Danny says that if Pablo goes knocking on Ousman's door, to give him a seeing-to, that as soon as Pablo goes inside Ousman'll be able to defend himself in all sorts of ways, that's where it could get dangerous, he could pick up a blunt instrument or a knife, Worst case and you're looking at someone getting killed, says Danny. And what if Ousman phones the police first and tells them you're standing outside his house, or his flat or his bedsit, or wherever he lives? If he hurts you then, he'll be able to say it was self-defence, it'll get him off the hook later on, says Danny.

Danny's head is shaved, with wounds here and there in his skull. Danny goes on and on, and his head is smooth and shiny, Pablo feels an urge to pass his hand over Danny's scalp, he's curious as to what a scalp feels like, whether it's soft or whether it's hard and dry and bumpy, like when you've just had a shave.

Give Ousman a warning, and leave it at that, says Danny.

The fight starts harmlessly enough. Pablo gives Ousman a slap in the face, Ousman snorts, he huffs and puffs (beats his chest). Pablo squares up, shoves his chest out (this too in the way of a beast), gives Ousman another slap, and that's when Ousman punches him, punches Pablo in the stomach, causing Pablo to drop to the floor. Ousman puts the boot in. He keeps on kicking for quite some time.

The next day, Ousman shows up at his mum's, and there, on the staircase in the building where his mum lives, he runs into the police, four uniformed and three in plain clothes, they detain him on the spot, they won't let him speak to his mum, who's locked the door from the inside. He knows she's standing looking at him through the spy hole. Two of the police officers go in to speak to her, two in plain clothes go away again, and the policewoman from before tells him to sit down on the stairs and wait. He sits there for hours, maybe three. Whenever a neighbour wants to get past, he has to stand up and step aside.

It's Friday and Pablo's slept into the morning on the sofa, curled up like a foetus, sleeping with his clothes on, his cap on his head, phone in hand, phone against his heart, the way a dog might sleep with a ball in its mouth. Pablo stirs, the lights are all on in the flat, his hands hurt and he can't remember why he's slept in his clothes, he can't remember where he is, and not a thing from the night before. He blinks and Danny's filthy flat comes into focus. He drinks from a half-empty coke bottle on the coffee table. And he remembers then, as he gulps down the coke, that last night, last night he could sense the time had come, the baby was on its way, and this was the first time Pablo understood anything at all to do with the baby, that the baby was going to come living into the world, that he was going to be a father, that the baby was going to grow up with him for a father.

Pablo sees the baby in his mind's eye, and then the thought is gone.

Pablo feels for the notes in his pocket, there they are, he thumbs through them, in his trouser pocket, counts them, twenty notes, twenty times five hundred kroner. He's completely forgotten he walked all the way home to Danny's place, walked with small wobbly steps along Trondheimsveien, not on the safe side with the new noise-reduction barrier, but on the other side where there's none, and consequently he staggered off the kerb more than once and could have been hit by a car. He walked, and his heart was thumping. He walked and felt paranoid, and his only thought was to get his hands on some more pills. He walked with his face turned towards the starry night sky, looking for the one constellation he knew, and eventually he found it. He gazed up at the stars and tuned in to the vibes they sent. And of course it was all too much for him. So Pablo lowered his head again and looked instead at the ground, looked at his phone, and sent Emily a text telling her she was the greatest thing in the universe, he told her he loved her more than all the universe, all the stars and planets put together.

It'd be easy to think all men had gone soft these days, that every man would jump to bring a cup of squash to a woman in labour, and so on, but Pablo lies to himself (his whole life of course is one big lie), he says he's not interested in any of that giving birth shit, screaming women with their legs in the air, I can see the kid some other time, I'll see the kid when this is over, he tells himself. He'll have some Fernet. Because wasn't it all just a fad, men having to be there when their women gave birth? It never used to be like that. They think they're getting something out of it, but they're not, Pablo concludes.

Pablo's short, his skin is yellow and sweaty. His mum says Pablo was always crawling between his brothers' legs and that's why he didn't grow any more than he did.

Pablo's a small person, it's something that weighs heavily on him even if he never tells anyone. Once when he was a kid Pablo repeatedly stabbed a knife into the bedroom door just because he felt he was short.

Pablo's spine curves inwards like the neck of a white swan, Emily often thinks about it. Emily's more hunched, with a thick neck, she forgets to hold her belly in when she's on the checkout, and sits too far forward on the chair.

Pablo actually works in the stores at Nortura's food processing plant where he operates a forklift and keeps tabs on the inventory (sometimes he'd come home with kilos of meat), but he tells people he works in the offices.

Back in the day, before he started lying about everything, Pablo was a meek and timid young man. Nearly all that's gone now, what's left of that other, weaker Pablo has been buried so deep he's as good as forgotten.

Well, all his life Pablo's been highly sensitive.

Well, typical Pablo to act like he's tough when actually he's scared.

Pablo's uncle said to him one day, when Pablo was crying about something, that Pablo had to start taking things like a man.

NOW HE'S A MAN

NOW HE MEETS EM

SAY HI AND SHE'S YOURS, PABLO

What was it about her? Who was she? Don't know. Because Em's not that gorgeous, she could have been, maybe, if her lips had been a bit fuller (so she reckons), but it's not her lips that are wrong, it's her forehead, her hairline's too low. He could catch himself staring at her for seconds at a time, there was something about her. Like what, well, like something, I don't know, sometimes a person can see something attractive where others can't, a certain look in the eyes, a quiet personality, for example, or big front teeth. He liked to watch her eat, the way she tried to hide her mouth, maybe it was her front teeth, he thought it was exactly like she was from Asia.

Boasting to Em when he first met her, Pablo showed her photos of his big living room: big coffee table; big, very thin TV. Everything's so big here! (She LOVES BIG THINGS, though for no reason in particular.) Look at this, and look at this, look at everything I've got, Em, I can buy you whatever you want. You can come over to mine anytime. This is how he talks to her in the beginning. She's just like a trophy, that's what he thinks, he'll be able to show her off. He picks her up from work, he drives her home. She says she loves him, she tells him so for the first time when the moment feels right, what sort of a moment, when they're out to eat / having a shag / a just-got-in-from-work moment, and when she tells him he kisses her. She tells him a lot after that first time, casually, in passing, when she's getting out of the car, only he's never able or doesn't want to tell her the same thing back.

And then she's pregnant, he's not ready for it, she wants money for a new TV, she wants to get her eyebrows microbladed (cost: 4K), she wants far, far too much.

Well, he doesn't need this.

Typically he'll take 100 g weed on the slate, pay back what he owes after selling it on, and keep the profit for his own habit. That way he breaks even, and if he'd kept on breaking even like that then Pablo might still have been living with Emily. Or maybe he wouldn't, a lot of fathers get distracted by other things, like other girls' cunts, anything to get away from a life of nappies. Who knows what Pablo's excuse was, maybe he just couldn't get his head round it. Maybe it was time to start a new chapter?

We don't really talk about Pablo having fathered a child and not wanting to see it.

He knows, he can feel it in his piss, that the baby's about to come out, and perhaps he also feels an urge to go and see them at the hospital. He asks after her, at the hospital, only they won't let him on the ward, not because he's scruffy and unwashed, but because he comes across as so uncertain, hugely uncertain. When he tells them he's the father, one of the nurses says, Aha, and asks him to wait. When she comes back, she says it's all right. He follows her into a room. Only that's not what happens at all, he doesn't go there, it'd only make matters worse, going to see the baby and then leaving them in the lurch later on. Pablo turns back on his way to the hospital, he changes his mind. What does he feel? No idea, I don't think he feels anything, I don't want to know.

Now Pablo sleeps, though not soundly: after a couple of hours he wakes with a start, clammy with sweat. Is he thinking about the baby?

GET OVER IT

So this is how her life is going to proceed from now on, but slowly slowly. She wonders for example when it's going to change, when what's going to change, when the baby's going to stop being a shell for example and become a person she can talk to. (And if Pablo's going to come and see his baby soon.)

It's snowing again as she comes out of the flats pushing the pram. Look at the flats, Emily, don't you hate the flats, and the grass at the front? The baby isn't asleep yet, but babbles to himself, and Em goes quickly down to the metro station where she walks up and down the platform to make the baby fall asleep before the train comes. When the display says one minute until the next train, the baby makes a crying sound and all Em's muscles tense in her body, she doesn't know how to ride the metro with a baby that's crying and so she turns round and goes back up the slope from the platform in the direction of the shopping precinct. It's half an hour's walk and the baby falls asleep after five minutes. Em walks quickly, pushing the pram with no gloves on.

There she is now, among the aisles at Lindex with her pram, looking at the children's clothes. Not that Liam (because that's his name) needs anything, but Em just seems to be able to let go of her thoughts when she's at Lindex, it's like she doesn't have to think at all when she's there (for no reason in particular), she feels herself relax, she can buy what she wants, buy clothes, put the clothes under the pram, and later, when she's got back home, put the new clothes on him. The light inside the precinct is yellow and in the middle of the day there's hardly anyone else there, a few other mums with prams, pensioners eating at the cafeteria, men of foreign background idling away their time. She goes through the other shops that sell children's things, she looks at nappy bags for the pram, and trousers and lacy little baby tops, before going into the supermarket and buying a coke, she nearly downs it in one, the bubbles tickle her throat and nose, she coughs, and then goes towards the toilets. One of the attendants has put a couple of chairs out in the passage, Em goes there to sit down and breastfeed, she digs a boob out and tries to get Liam to feed. He cries for a time, women go past on their way to the loo and stare, until eventually his mouth clamps around the nipple. Em tips her head back, her eyes look at nothing in particular and now she feels dizzy.

EMILY'S SO YOUNG, SHE'S SO YOUNG that she doesn't know anything about life, it scares me.

Completely oblivious to her life being a sweet lie, she slips with ease into the role of the single mother that on paper she's been from the start.

She goes to the precinct several times a week. She thinks about money (though for no reason in particular), and instead of gazing out of her window with that distant look in her eyes, the way she probably should, she texts BALANCE to 2100 to see if any more money's come in. Someone, guess who, has transferred 10,000 into her account today. She spends what's left of the day moving the money between her accounts, and it's so satisfying to see, to look at the figure and see that the money is there.

What does she love?

She loves her money, she loves making her face up, she loves watching TV, she loves Liam (though for the moment she's forgotten all about him), she's moving towards not loving Pablo anymore, only she doesn't know it yet.

Before Liam came she had a piercing in her belly button, but that was then, the midwife had to tell her (with a look of disdain) to "take that out." She steps over to the mirror and looks at herself. She finds her belly ring and puts it back in again, wets a cotton bud in her mouth and wipes away the black smudge made by her fluttering eyelashes, stands a moment and dances while looking at herself, really? well, why not, it's what young girls do, and then she takes some photos of herself, sends them to Pablo and saves them in a folder with some others.

Now it's time to join a mothers' group, something she's been trying to avoid for some time, she hasn't even put her name down on the list at the health centre, and so it comes as a bit of a shock when she discovers someone's phoned. It's her mum who takes the call, they want to know if Emily's coming to their meeting. Em's mum tells them Em's in the shower and can't come to the phone, but yes, she's coming to the meeting. Em's got no say in the matter, she's not even asked, and it feels like she's being kicked out of her own flat when her mum packs the nappy bag and gets Liam into his woollens while telling Em to get a move on. Bitch, Em says under her breath as she puts her shoes on. What was that? says her mum. Nothing, says Em. We should teach Liam to nap outside in his pram soon, says Em's mum, shouldn't we, she says to Liam, holding him in her arms while Em puts her coat and hat on. Mum, you can't teach a three-month-old baby where to sleep, says Em.

She's not had a chance to think about it before she's in the lift with Liam in his pram. He's quiet today and falls asleep straight away. She wonders if there's something wrong when he's like that. They take the metro, two stops, she's on edge even though he's asleep, then finds the housing block where the group's having their meeting. She rings the bell and the woman who lives there comes to the door, puts out her hand, and says her name's June. The other mothers (old) who've already arrived wave to Em and Liam as they step into the living room. Em sits down on the floor with Liam.

She sits and listens to the others as they talk, about cars, about decorating, about books, things that are totally beyond her. One of the mothers has brought a nice purply-red book with her about what it's like to have a baby. It gets passed around. Em skims through it, reads a single sentence, then puts it down again (books aren't for people like you, Emily). The woman who said her name was June says that sometimes it feels almost like there's no one else in the world who's ever had a baby. Another mother says she feels so strong for having given birth.

There's cake and coffee, and a salad too. Em doesn't get round to having anything, but sits on the floor throughout with Liam, holding him to her chest, if he isn't lying on his back on a mat in front of her. She hardly says a word, says nothing, in fact, until it's time to go (on her way home she has to stop off and buy herself a hot dog, she's nearly dying of starvation).

This is how her days go by …

But we can't leave her in the lurch, not when she's as vulnerable as this.

She needs some joy in her life, the way she's living now all she's doing is breathing through that narrow nose of hers, in and out.

Look at her pushing the pram, this invisible could-be-anyone person on her way to the metro station. Her baby's in a sleeping bag that's far too warm for him, she bought it with her benefit money (but benefits aren't proper money, and your baby's going to start crying soon, so don't be too glad, Emily). On the metro she thinks for a moment it's Pablo she sees at one of the other stops. Pablo sitting on a bench wearing jeans and a cap, perhaps trying to hide from her?

She wanders around the precinct, takes off her coat and tucks it under the pram, Liam's crying again, crying all the time, in his uncomfortably warm sleeping bag, and she has to go and sit down on the chair in the passage outside the toilets. She picks her boiling-hot baby up out of his pram, removes some of his layers, he's still crying, then puts him back in the pram for a second so she can pull her T-shirt up in such a way that her breast will still be hidden when she feeds him. Or actually no, she pulls her T-shirt down, from the collar, and her boob plops out, she can't work out how to breastfeed discreetly.

She needs a friend, a girl in the same situation, a guiding light, to measure herself against.

Yes, and now another young mum appears with her pram in the same shops as Em frequents, that's where she sees her, all of a sudden she's there, and what a lot of equipment she's got with her, underneath the pram, and a bag hanging from the hook on the side of the pram, a coke in the cup holder. At first, Em notices this other mum because they're about the same age, then, after having gone past each other on different days, four times in all, Em notices her earrings, big gold earrings, and her high, thick ponytail, her pearly skin (exceptionally pure skin) and red lips.

The other mum's baby is lying in its pram with the canopy pushed back, lying awake in its pram calm as you like, without crying, something Liam never does, and for that reason Em often carries him around the precinct in a baby carrier.

In the passage Em now thinks of as her breast-feeding spot, the other mum, producing a big maternity pillow she then places on her lap and tucks around her waist, starts talking to her. Her baby's bigger than Em's and she asks Em how old Em's baby is. Em says that Liam's fourteen weeks, and the girl's face lights up. Mine's sixteen weeks, she says, and greedy for his milk. So Em asks her how often she feeds him, it's the first thing she's ever asked about since Liam came, and the other mum says her baby wants feeding about every two hours. He's very efficient, he swallows after every suck, the other mum says, and Em looks down at her own son, who doesn't swallow until his whole mouth's full, and she says, This one here's very efficient too.

She imagines the other mum driving to the precinct in her car, the other mum lifting her baby out of his pram and securing him in the baby seat, one of those that can be rotated to face sideways, the other mum folding the pram and putting it in the boot and driving home to her husband, to her house, to her bathroom with its many drawers and jewellery boxes, that's where she puts her earrings. In the mornings, Em imagines, the other mum wakes up before her baby and has her breakfast before lifting him up and feeding him, and after that she changes his nappy and washes him. (Emily, you do wash Liam in the mornings as well, don't you?) She tickles her baby on the changing table and says "quality time" out loud. Afterwards, the baby sits in a baby bouncer on the floor while she puts her makeup on, while she gets dressed, while she ties her shoes. Then she picks the baby up and puts a little hat on him and goes out to the car, secures the baby in his baby seat, and drives to the precinct to meet Em.

The other mum asks what Em's husband does, and Em says she hasn't got one, she's on her own. Did you have him on your own? the other mum asks. Yes, we broke up before he was born, says Em, and the other mum lets out a little Oh no, while smiling at the same time, and after that she says, You must be really strong, in a way that's perhaps meant to be a comfort, but which nonetheless casts Emily as weak, the way utterances like that make a person shrink, a top-down thing to say, that suggests Emily's not only weak, but stupid too. But I think Liam's better off with me being on my own, says Em. He doesn't cry, for example, when I'm getting myself ready in the bathroom. Which isn't true, of course: at this point she ought to have told the other mum how Liam cried from five in the morning till half past seven as he tried to press out his poo, how Emily eventually had to play white noise at full volume on her phone and put it down next to Liam in his cot and shut him inside the bedroom while he screamed, because she had to have a shower. How Liam cries as soon as she puts him down on the changing table, the way his body goes all stiff, and Em's ended up not changing his nappy as often as before, only when it's full of poo, and only then after some time. He can lie in a nappy full of poo for up to an hour, his botty'll be all red and shiny then.

Some days Liam can be quite helpless, with his big tummy and his twiggy little insect legs, he won't stop screaming, his tum's full of wind and his belly button's swollen, the nurse draws attention to it when they go for his checkup, Em says Liam keeps pressing but can't press anything out. Em can look at Liam's big tummy, and she can press it gently too, but she doesn't know what it's supposed to feel like. Em inserts a thermometer into his rectum, it was what the nurse did at his checkup, and a lot of poo comes out when she does, and Liam settles down a bit. Liam cries too because he doesn't want Em to put a sweater on him, is that what it is, he's only fifteen weeks old, how can he not want his clothes putting on, she can't understand it. Emily's tired, she's hungry, she grips Liam by the arm, lifts him up by the arm, too hard she realises afterwards, because Liam screams and her forefinger leaves a bruise.

And it happens too that Liam is neglected, but that's a few months from now, Liam lies or sits on his own on the floor all day in front of the television, while Emily's asleep in her bed, in her own room, she can't be bothered getting up, because all Liam does is scream at the top of his lungs.

Is it all right to say now that if Emily had still been with Pablo she'd have died?

But what would she have died of, I don't understand what you mean. It's Liam talking now, he's got to wonder why he was even put in the world, why his mum didn't swallow the pill she was given by the nurse at the outpatient clinic, and the other ones later on, to squeeze him out into the toilet bowl. I don't understand why I haven't got a proper dad , why I've been totally rejected.

She understands him too when she looks at him, at Liam, that helpless child, he hardly ever opens his eyes, but sucks and sucks at her breast, and if he's not sleeping or feeding, he's crying, it gets her frustrated, she had no idea newborn babies cried this much. She can see, when Liam lies on the pillow in her lap with her boob in his mouth, how his little body relaxes and that he feels completely secure with her.

She promises Liam that she'll always be there for him, that she'll look after him, Liam's going to have a totally different life from now on. She's amazed at herself, that she could have such maternal feelings inside her, that some part of her is actually a mother. And she can lie there with her baby on her tummy, she must lie completely flat on the sofa, and her baby will sleep on her tummy, they can lie there for hours together.

And then there's this new friend she's made at the precinct, her name's Alexa, she's got a name now, they've had coffee together at the precinct and she wants Em and Liam to come and visit her. Em spends a lot of time thinking about Alexa, when Liam's asleep on top of her she can vanish completely into thoughts about the things Alexa does, because Alexa does everything so gracefully, in a way that appeals to her, if that's all right to say. The way she hangs her coat nicely over the back of the chair before she sits down, instead of clutching it in her lap, for example, or tossing it into the pram, or the way her mouth falls back into the most natural duck face after she's been talking. Alexa texted Em to ask if they'd like to come round on Friday, it was Monday then, and she texted her again Thursday to make sure. Em felt how her heart started beating. Now they're on the bus, Liam's asleep and Em's sitting on the fold-down seat in the space that's reserved for prams. She's listening to music. The sun shines through the bus windows and dazzles her completely. She hasn't just done her brows, she's done her lashes as well, she was thinking about Alexa, because she wants Alexa to notice and pass comment, and Alexa says, after Em's taken off her coat and lifted Liam out of the pram, Your brows are really gorgeous. Thanks a lot, says Em, and Alexa adds, You have got really good brows though.

They sit on the sofa, the babies are lying on the floor next to each other under a baby gym, and Liam looks and looks, how quiet he is, at the new toys that dangle above him. Em's never known him to be so quiet and now she wants to buy exactly the same baby gym for him, Where did you get it, she asks

Alexa. And Alexa says it was a present from someone, but you can get them anywhere (these are the sort of things they talk about). Em picks Liam up off the floor and puts him on her knee, though Liam's too small yet to sit on a knee, his back goes all curved, his head wobbles and drops slackly forward.

Alexa fetches two more cokes. You must be dead strong, she says. I don't understand how you can manage. She leans across the table, leans in such a way (with urgency) that she looks like she's about to take Em's hands. What happened, did he just leave you, did he give you any indication beforehand? I don't know, says Em, and she doesn't either. Could you feel anything beforehand, did you have any idea? I don't know, and she doesn't, she doesn't know where Alexa's going with all these questions, why's she asking her all these things. She starts to laugh and says she's never thought of herself as a typical single mum. Alexa says it's not funny, that she ought to sue her bloke and get some money out of him, if you can sue people for that, you must be able to, surely? Probably, says Em, I haven't a clue.

And then she's back on the stuffy, packed-out bus again, and it's almost like Alexa's put a brand-new shiny thought in her head. She's never thought of herself as ... a single mum before. She doesn't feel old though, she's always thought of single mums as old. For a second she's scared about what might happen to her face and body, scared that everything's going to go loose and flabby. And she doesn't really know what a dad is either, or what kind of a role a dad's supposed to play, she thinks it'd be something like carrying things up the stairs, mending the pram, changing nappies, etc.

Somebody's got to sign the paternity acknowledgement (not that great to see Father unknown on your birth certificate), but in the absence of male role models and father figures in this world there's still no name on the document.

Em explains to Liam she was so desperate that in a moment of grief and despondency (I just sat there crying) she was about to ask the neighbour if he'd mind if she put his name on it, just until Pablo signed his own. Em says the neighbour was very much in love with her, she says so to give herself a boost, it makes her feel really strong to say something like that out loud.

It should have been the neighbour who put his name on the paternity acknowledgement, he'd have been so good for them, he'd have looked after them, even if it had only have been for a few months.

The neighbour would have signed the document with hardly a moment's hesitation, he can't ever think straight when he gets flustered, he acts on instinct, and it never helps much anyway to think things through.

She could have rung his doorbell one evening, that's how it could have happened, and explained to him: He comes to the door, she's standing there, about to explain (Em, you're making this up, it's all in your imagination). What does Em look like? Her face is all blotchy, the way it is when a person's been crying, and her hair's all greasy too, she's got a sickly sweet smell, the neighbour thinks. It's the milk that smells, but the neighbour doesn't know that, he's never smelled a mother's milk before (only when he was little, and he can't remember that). She explains everything to him, that she was going out with Pablo, but now Pablo's left her and wants no part in the baby's life. It's probably a good idea not to have a criminal father involved, but the baby has a right to a father according to the authorities, because of course you can't have a baby without one, and if the father won't sign the papers it means someone else has to do it, and so she was thinking he might, it's only a formality. All this is explained with great hesitancy, standing in his hallway. She says that if it's all right with him, he can sign right away, just so there's a name, so it can all go through, and later on everything's bound to sort itself out.

He can be a father for nearly six months, until Pablo acknowledges paternity. He can walk the floor bouncing Liam in his arms many times during those few months, he can push Liam around the block in his pram.

And Liam'll forget his keys when he goes off to school, it happens all the time, there's no one place for keys in the flat, so often when they're going out somewhere Em'll go back and forth swearing and shouting while searching for her keys, in a way that frightens Liam: What are you staring at, she'll say, and jab a finger at him, at little Liam, when all he's doing is standing there. And anyway, Liam's so little he of course forgets where he puts things (one time after swimming he can't find his clothes in the changing room and has to wear his rain set the rest of the day at school with nothing on underneath).

Liam rings the neighbour's doorbell and the neighbour comes to the door, he lets him into his flat and fries two eggs.

Liam eats the eggs sitting at the table, the neighbour eats too and is about to ask Liam how everything's going, but instead he asks what time Emily's coming home, and Liam says, I don't know, pause, Liam says she always comes home late, after which the neighbour clears his throat and says the grown-ups have to go to work and that Emily goes to work for Liam's sake, while Liam jiggles his legs under the table and shifts about on his chair, and the neighbour pours him some more coke, which Liam drinks.

When Liam's four months old Pablo is obliged by the authorities to take a DNA test.

Did he have to go to the hospital, to a designated department at the hospital, and have his blood tested? Did a nurse roll up his sleeve, tighten a band around his arm, and carefully insert a needle into his vein? I hope she messed it up and needed several stabs at it, that it hurt and left him bruised.

Then a letter arrives in the post, she has to open it, and it says that Pablo is the father, that the child has such and such a blood type, that the child was born in such and such a place, that the child is entitled to such and such an amount of money. By then her mum's already helped her get in touch with NAV, which is the social welfare agency, she's asked NAV to order him to take a DNA test with a view to determining his paternity, and if he doesn't do that there'll be an injunction, it can end up in the courts, fucking NAV, all those phone calls and meetings with NAV, Em's mum sitting beside her when she's had to talk to them on the phone, Em's mum stroking Em's cheek afterwards.

I need to tell you something now, Liam, and you might want to sit down on your chair. Sit on your chair. No, on second thoughts, come and sit on my lap. Come here and sit with me, Liam! Your dad's away working, he works a long way away and can't come and collect you from nursery school this week. Your dad lives in a different city. Your dad lives in a foreign country. No, that's not your dad! Your dad's out there somewhere, I don't know where. I'm trying to shield you from him. He won't be coming back. He's not cut out for being a family, he took off to live another life. When you're old enough you might be able to meet him one day. Your dad was a very diffi-cult man, I couldn't depend on him, and I think that if we'd stayed together I'd have gone mad. I was upset for a very long time, you don't get over a per-son just like that, you can't just flick a switch and forget all about them, can you? I'll probably never get over it, not really, I don't suppose you ever do get over your first love, or get over being … abandoned, does that sound right?

What does a man look like who meets his child for the first time when the child is no longer a naked screaming infant, but has become a chubby, or perhaps a rather wiry, ruddy-cheeked seven-year-old, I honestly haven't a clue.

Because later Liam will have to meet Pablo, or his father (as he's referred to now) at McDonald's or some such place. And when he does it'll be something Em and his father have agreed on beforehand over the phone, that it's okay for Liam to meet him. Em says that Liam has a right to know where he comes from. His father says he's fine with that and that he'd like to get to know his son. So now you want to know your son, Em thinks to herself, but says nothing, what's the point of arguing after six years. And they agree then on McDonald's, because that's the sort of place kids like.

Liam's maybe seven years old and looks at his dad. Liam's dad looks at Liam. They don't know each other, Liam hadn't imagined his dad would be that short, and he doesn't like it either. His dad goes on and on about his job, he says he's in something called inventory management. Liam doesn't understand what his dad's talking about while he's talking about his job. His dad's got some presents for him, action figures and robots, that sort of thing. He wants to take Liam's hands in his. He leans across the table, bends over Liam like an old man, to take his son's hands in his.

Em comes and collects Liam at 7 p.m., his dad stays behind at the bus stop and waves. Liam twists round on the seat to look back at him, one last wave, it's awkward for such a little boy, he's spent a couple of hours with a man who's basically a stranger. He walks from the bus with his mum, and when they come in, close to bedtime, he says it felt a bit weird, and Em says, But Liam, you got so many nice new toys (very expensive). And Liam gets into bed, Em tucks him in, sleep time.

Look, now Em and Liam emerge from the bedroom, they go into the kitchen, Em puts Liam in his bouncy chair, it's a baby chair and he's getting to be a big boy now, perhaps he'll be able to sit up properly on his own soon, but for the time being he can lie in his bouncy chair. He lies there looking, what he sees I don't know, if he can even see at all, if everything isn't just a blur to him. She gives Liam little chunks of banana while she eats a yoghurt. And now look, she can smile, she couldn't do that only a few days ago. She smiles at her baby, and before long, maybe not now, but soon, her baby will smile back.

In no time at all Liam's become a big chubby baby, five hundred grams a week he's been putting on, he's gone from three to nine kilos. He's so big now the midwife looks at his growth curve as if it can't be right, she raises her eyebrows and says My goodness and asks if he's getting anything more than just milk. You are just breastfeeding him, aren't you, you're not giving him formula? Emily nods, she rocks her little boy and says, There's nothing wrong with him, is there? No, not at all, the midwife says, his weight's just been going up very quickly, he's quite strapping for four months. How often do you feed him? Em doesn't know, they've got no routines, she says every three hours, which isn't true, when they're at home she offers him a boob at least once an hour, just to make him shut up. The midwife says everything's fine. She just wants to measure his head before she goes, to make sure he hasn't got water on the brain. Em doesn't know what that is, and doesn't dare ask, she sees dreadful images in her mind of little children with massive heads.

She has to run to catch the bus home, pushing the pram as she goes, straight out onto the pedestrian crossing. She manages to bang on the side of the bus, and shouts too for the driver to wait, before it pulls away and leaves her there. The driver must have seen her, surely? A girl with a pram, it's even got a nappy bag attached. The cheek of it, have you ever heard the like?

So she walks along the stupid road in the direction of the woods. She walks on the pavement. It's hot today, she's sweaty and glistens in the sun. They're going to meet Alexa and her baby, to go for a walk in the woods, they'll push their prams along the track in the woods. Emily's hardly ever been for a walk, she's a city girl, she doesn't know what woods are. She walks along on the warm tarmac, pushing the pram. She knows this tarmac, she can feel it on her cheek.

The pastor's still there in his flat. He was afraid she'd take a fall on the stairs with that big belly of hers, but she didn't. Em's still in her own flat with her baby, or she's out with the baby in his pram. Of course, she doesn't take the stairs anymore, she takes the lift, and if the lift's out of order she doesn't go out at all, that must be it, because he hardly ever sees her these days. All he can do is imagine. He'll vanish soon, not die, but disappear out of her life, because now he's no use to her.

Now's when infatuation from afar turns into ... something genuine?

Do you fancy going out sometime?

Do you fancy going out to eat at a proper restaurant, not just a cafeteria?

If you like?

He turns it all over in his mind.

I'm getting on a bit, but what would it matter, if I had a young girlfriend like that?

He decides to ask her out.

He takes the lift up to hers, no, he takes the stairs, a person takes the stairs when they're nervous, and he's very nervous, it's at the back of his mind the whole time how he comes across, if he smiles it's wrong and if he doesn't smile it's wrong, he tries to make his face relax, his hands are clammy. He wonders what he looks like, he wonders how old Emily is, he doesn't know, he thinks maybe she's twenty-four (she isn't). How old is he, exactly? Probably twice her age. He steps up to her door and rings the bell, no, he knocks (let's not hope he rings the bell, it could wake the baby), and she comes to the door, she's wearing jeans and a sweater, she steps out onto the landing, not wanting to ask him in (she'd have to sleep with him then) and she doesn't quite get what he wants, she doesn't grasp this at all as he stands there and starts to explain himself. The pastor, or Jan, tells her he's ... he thinks they had such a nice time at the cafeteria that day and he was wondering if ... no, now he doesn't know what to say. She stands facing him, open, waiting to hear what he's going to say. He says something about the cafeteria and something about help, if she needs any help, if it gets to be too much on her own, all she has to do is say the word, he likes kids, he's heard her baby crying, often for a long time, it doesn't bother him, but ... But what? But maybe other people can't get to sleep, for example, maybe someone'll complain. He just wanted to talk to her, and maybe, if she wants, maybe they could go out for a decent meal together one day.

She gets that he sees something, and for a moment she almost sees it too.

All she can do is agree with him, yes, yes, yes, she can hardly do otherwise, she can't say no, can she?

He steps towards her and now he's far too close to her face (not what he intended), so close that she, that probably she can smell his breath, or at least see everything, his scars, his skin, his beard, the follicles from which his beard grows (he's that old).

Yes, Em surely knows what he wants, he's sent her notes, or just the one, but she never replied, and anyway it's often her mother who empties her letter box, he might have sent more than one, we don't know, and did she even realise that it was he who'd sent it? She was just trying to be nice to him at that cafeteria, she hadn't given out any signals that it was anything other than that, or had she? I don't know, she doesn't know, all she does is stand there agape.

He tries to kiss her on the mouth, and he does too, and when he kisses her he lets out a little noise that sounds like a cat when it starts to purr.

He canters back down the stairs and perhaps feels very stupid, or very relieved, sometimes it's a relief when things come to nothing, and this was nothing much at all really, was it?

Em stands in the doorway after he's gone down the stairs. She has no idea now what she thinks.

She's been asleep on the sofa, on her back, not in the foetal position, or has she, maybe she was just resting a bit, with her eyes closed, not asleep, but thinking. How funny that someone would want her, that this pastor, or whatever he is, wants to go to bed with her, nothing like it has ever happened to her before, it makes her fingers warm and tingly, a warmth in her back too, even though she doesn't want him (too old, probably far too careful with her, if she did go to bed with him), and even though this could almost have been a case of inappropriate behaviour, or sexual misconduct (!?) there's a warmth all the way down her legs, it feels like she's won something.

I'll leave her now. She's not going to die, she's got Liam, and she won't leave Liam in the shopping precinct either, as was the idea. She's going to close her eyes, she's very, very tired, and often drops off for a bit when she's lying on the floor with her baby.

This will buoy her up now for quite a while, won't it? Little explosions inside, all to herself.

ACKNOWLEDGEMENTS

The quotes on pages 24 and 128 are from Kirsten Thorup's 2016 novel *Erindring om kærligheden* ("Recollection of Love"). In the present novel one of those quotes has been slightly rephrased.

The third chapter takes its title from the song "Jobb, penger og helse" by Åsmund Sem-Johansen.

The final chapter takes its title from the song "Kom deg over" by Beglomeg.

Some elements of the chapter about Pablo were sourced at www.freak.no.

Thanks to Geir Gulliksen and Signe Russwurm at Forlaget Oktober.

MARTIN AITKEN's translations of contemporary Scandinavian literature are numerous. His work has appeared on the shortlists of the International DUBLIN Literary Award and the US National Book Awards, as well as the 2021 International Booker Prize. He received the PEN America Translation Prize in 2019, and most recently the 2022 US National Translation Award in Prose. He lives and works in Denmark.

Book Club Discussion Guides on our website.

World Editions promotes voices from around the globe by publishing books from many different countries and languages in English translation. Through our work, we aim to enhance dialogue between cultures, foster new connections, and open doors which may otherwise have remained closed.

Also available from World Editions:

Breakwater
Marijke Schermer
Translated by Liz Waters
"A poignant story of love, autonomy, and the devastating power of secrets." —IVO VAN HOVE

Afterlight
Jaap Robben
Translated by David Doherty
"Deals with all kinds of inflammable material with such tact and understanding." —HILARY MANTEL

Fowl Eulogies
Lucie Rico
Translated by Daria Chernysheva
"Disturbing, compelling, and hearbreaking."
—CYNAN JONES, author of *The Dig*

My Mother Says
Stine Pilgaard
Translated by Hunter Simpson
"A hilarious queer break-up story."
—OLGA RAVN, author of *The Employees*

We Are Light
Gerda Blees
Translated by Michele Hutchison
"Beautiful, soulful, rich, and relevant."
—*Libris Literature Prize*

On the Design

As book design is an integral part of the reading experience, we would like to acknowledge the work of those who shaped the form in which the story is housed.

Tessa van der Waals (Netherlands) is responsible for the cover design, cover typography, and art direction of all World Editions books. She works in the internationally renowned tradition of Dutch Design. Her bright and powerful visual aesthetic maintains a harmony between image and typography, and captures the unique atmosphere of each book. She works closely with internationally celebrated photographers, artists, and letter designers. Her work has frequently been awarded prizes for Best Dutch Book Design.

The cover image was shot by Ryoji Iwata, an architect and photographer based in Tokyo. Iwata takes photos on an iPhone, an approach to photography which he says changed his life. He used glass and water droplets to create the bokeh, or blur, effect.

The typeface used for the title on the cover is Jute, a military-inspired font created by YouWorkForThem. Cover designer Tessa van der Waals selected this square font because she appreciated the way the lowercase stroke of the y continues visually in the stroke of the lowercase r. The font used for the author's name is Neutraface Text, designed by House Industries and named after the architect Richard Neutra.

The cover has been edited by lithographer Bert van der Horst of BFC Graphics (Netherlands).

Euan Monaghan (United Kingdom) is responsible for the typography and careful interior book design.

The text on the inside covers and the press quotes are set in Circular, designed by Laurenz Brunner (Switzerland) and published by Swiss type foundry Lineto.

All World Editions books are set in the typeface Dolly, specifically designed for book typography. Dolly creates a warm page image perfect for an enjoyable reading experience. This typeface is designed by Underware, a European collective formed by Bas Jacobs (Netherlands), Akiem Helmling (Germany), and Sami Kortemäki (Finland). Underware are also the creators of the World Editions logo, which meets the design requirement that "a strong shape can always be drawn with a toe in the sand."

Printed in the USA
CPSIA information can be obtained
at www.ICGtesting.com
JSHW020717060524
62535JS00001B/1